Piranesi's Figures

PIRANESI'S FIGURES

HANNAH CALDER

NEW STAR BOOKS Vancouver 2016

Piranesi's Figures is a work of fiction. Any resemblance by any character to any person, living or dead, is entirely coincidental.

The publisher acknowledges the financial support of the Canada Council for the Arts, the Government of Canada through the Canada Book Fund, the British Columbia Arts Council, and the Province of British Columbia through the Book Publishing Tax Credit.

Cataloguing information for this book is available from Library and Archives Canada, collectionscanada.gc.ca

Printed & bound in Canada on 100% post-consumer recycled paper by Imprimerie Gauvin, Gatineau, QC

ISBN 978-1-55420-112-9
Cover design by Oliver McPartlin
Typeset by New Star Books
First printing, May 2016

NEW STAR BOOKS LTD
#107–3477 Commercial St, Vancouver, BC V5N 4E8 CANADA
1574 Gulf Road, #1517 Point Roberts, WA 98281 USA
newstarbooks.com · info@newstarbooks.com

For the displaced dreamers
and their displaced dreams

somewhere the small green
weeds hover in the cement cracks, waiting to return earth
to her rightful promise.

Rita Wong, *forage*

Prologue

IT WAS THE KIND OF DREAM THAT COULD FILL A BOOK. In all caps the word NINEVEH appeared. Just like that. Straight out of the pit of Jung's lungs. A menorah was there too, candle-free, out of service.

JONAH'S HAIR IS LONG AND BLACK, shiny like the wet skin of a killer whale. He wears sandals and has a tea-towel over his head held in place by a piece of string that I found in the shed. His skin is pale like the eyelashes of the nativity play angel that taunts me with her blonde ambition.

The whale blubber in the black and white encyclopedia looks cozy enough, but if it is like the scum that rises from the pan of boiling animal parts that stinks up my grandfather's house and makes his four dogs slobber, I would not want to live in it for three days and three nights.

But a split-open whale is different to a live one ploughing through kelp and creatures, lit up by Pinocchio's match, water sloshing in and out and up and down its breathy bones. Jonah lives in the whale's belly for three days and three nights.

A miracle! When he emerges he is gut covered, painted the colour of blood, raisined at the fingers and toes.

THE DREAM DOES ITS JOB. Then it leaves in its place a hole where a story can burrow in and root itself. An empty skull, shaken free of its weird and hard to explain or remember images, brain stuff scooped out.

The unconscious, long whistled back to the collective pool where it can recharge and enter another newborn's head, houses the dream story. It sits on a mossy mound open to the four winds, the thousand rains, the one sun, open to the once-upon-a-time and happily-ever-after that mate with violent persistence inside the writer's head.

One

FLORENCE IS STILL ALIVE. Very old, but living in a seaside nursing home with all her faculties and trinkets about her. Big deal that Stephen cheated on her fifty-odd years ago. There are so many memories that beat that one out for her attention. She focuses on the good old days and the day-to-day. Bingo, prunes and custard, Brian the manager dressed as Father Christmas, Jenny's wedding, whether the sparrows are being outsmarted by the starlings and going hungry because of it, what brooch to wear for Sunday roast, whether Paddy has a thing for her or whether he prefers Lily.

It is a dark afternoon, rain on the horizon, skulking closer. Florence is gazing out the window at an August picnic. She sees her little brother running towards her shouting that there's a bull in the field; then suddenly everyone is scrambling over the gate with jelly legs and potato salad sliding off their plates.

"Hi, Gran."

Florence looks up. Her granddaughter, Mia. Smiling.

"Mia. Come on in."

Mia barely squeezes into the room because she is carrying so much baggage from *The Italian Saga*, her current gig. After rummaging around in one of her bags she pulls out a coffee table art book. *Vedute di Roma: The Etchings of Giambattista Piranesi.*

Mia thinks she is thoughtful to bring her grandmother some art to look at—maybe she'll take up drawing?—but instead she ends up just depressing poor Gran in her darkening winter room with its baby blue nylon curtains that she brought from home to try to take the edge off.

Florence cannot draw to save her life. "Draw me a dog and I won't kill you!" shouts the killer. "Oh, no," says Florence. "I can't draw."

I can mother.

I can grandmother.

I can great-grandmother, if necessary.

But I can't draw.

MIA PLACES THE BOOK ON FLORENCE'S LAP and leans over the arm of the chair to flip the pages. The images are dark and uninviting to a woman used to kittens in vases, dogs smoking pipes. But Mia is excited and tells Florence that there is an exhibition of Piranesi's work on right now in Berlin. "I'm going to go there this weekend with my boyfriend—he's an artist too—to get inspiration for my final project."

Florence doesn't like the idea of Mia traveling, even with a boy.

"Most people are interested in the buildings, but I'm obsessed with these figures here. Look. Look at them. They all have walking sticks and they're wearing rags. What's that about?"

"I wouldn't know, dear."

Two

THEY SPEND THE AFTERNOON in the warmth of each other. In conversation. Mia brushes Florence's hair with one of those silver-backed brushes that seem merely decorative. Not this one. It does the trick in our grandmother's knotless tuft. Mia can hear people chatting, laughing, getting louder in the hallway. She puts the brush down and goes to the door. When she opens it she sees that all the characters have arrived and are waiting to come in.

Hilda and Jorgen enter first, holding hands for the first time in months. Hilda carries all her secrets behind her mouth. You know the type. You want to pry her open even though you already know what's inside. She has come straight from the hairdresser's, because like weddings and mid-winter dance parties, novels warrant getting your hair styled.

Jorgen looks out at the room from under the porch hangings of his eyelids. Torn from a gay wank mag; ripped at the arms and stomach; chiseled at the jawbone. He is shot from all angles by some pervert I refuse to abandon. Kept at the bay of my fingers, sheet scrunched inside the fist of a woman's bed, he makes a husband for a wife. For Hilda.

They are followed by Dr. Hans Grebing and his permanent

field trip of artists, plucked from the foreground of a Piranesi etching.

Once, the doctor's artists had been the stars of this show, but there was no knowing when they might slide into an outburst, slip into a coma of sadness, a revelry of delusions. There was no way of knowing when they might fall off the wagon into the arms of those heroin stars that wash over us like music. There was no way of knowing when they might turn into girls interrupted and start covering their hands with their too-long sleeves.

Mia holds her breath. She hadn't expected the Piranesi crowd to show up here.

The placement of these figures in the compositional field, always leaning, always lean, will not do for the purposes of entertainment. The quiet lull of the static, etched body must be replaced by a woman, wild with rage, tearing down Main Street in bare feet, in winter, in northern Canada, on the coldest day of the year. For Hollywood. For Entertainment.

But not here.

Mia's boyfriend gifted her with a stack of postcards when he got back from his Grand Tour. "Look at these guys!" he says. "So insignificant. Like you." These pinky-fingernail-sized guttersnipes; these scab-encrusted, unwashed dreamers; these human beings.

But she doesn't have a clue what it feels like to be a figure, a prop. Her trauma-tank holds nothing but the fumes of a few melodramatic rows with her mother, a few pervy winks from her dad, a few uneaten peanut butter sandwiches, stuffed in between rocks on her walk home from school.

She is here, free, off the street, running through the tall grass, remembering the Facebook post about what to do if a tick gets on you and starts burrowing in; locking her own door with her own key rifled from her own bag; soaping her own crotch. She is here, free, unaware of the dangers of alleyways, the seeping spit of puddle-water into old shoes, unaware of the seasons slapping against her makeshift cardboard line-ups for food.

The figures don't know where they'll end up. In what stories. What poems. Where they'll be hung out to drip significance on the coiffed hair of contest judges, on what clothesline, with what type of peg, in what foul breeze. It's all about the nouns, Mia thinks. Person. Place. Thing. It's the nouns that make headlines out of abandoned lives. The dates. The room numbers. The social services records filed under dementia schizophrenia. It's about the shell of the old city turned into a place to hide.

The surnames of the figures have been run over by the tires of the military vehicle that hums in the courtyard to the smell of cigarette smoke. The sound of men talking in voices belonging to soldiers in WWII films. It's all about the asylum, after it shut down, and the matter of the clang of the gas chamber door. The patient's body broken into sections for the ease of the catalogue. This section is damaged. A fall from a horse. Always a fall from a horse. This section is gone to the world. This section is catatonic.

MIA WHISPERS TO PIRANESI that *Vedute di Roma* has just started. The figures will be needed there. "It's OK," he says. "They're not staying long." She is relieved. There is no knowing what kind of clichés they might be infected with.

NEXT COME BILL, Violet, and Stephen, a trio of all things wrong with marriage and poverty. Bill holds a tape recorder, close to his chest, not wanting anyone else to press PLAY, STOP, or, most importantly, REWIND. Tucked between her two men, Violet, Queen of the Yellow Curtains, shy and vicious old badger, feels rather special. Bill is a teddy bear leaking stuffing, quick to smile, quick to shout. His adopted brother Stephen is, O the Unfairness of Life! younger by five years, fitter by ten laps, and less inclined to enter the wrong answers, in pen, to crossword clues.

Stephen kisses his wife Florence on the forehead and hands her the TV guide and a jumbo packet of licorice allsorts.

All the children come next. They hover around Florence with their palms cupped until she fills each finger-bowl with sweets.

Lastly comes Piranesi. He waits at the door, leaning against the door frame with his arms crossed like he owns this book, which he kind of does.

Three

MOST OF THE CHARACTERS FIND PLACES TO SIT. There aren't enough chairs, so some perch on the radiator, others on the windowsill. A few hop up onto Florence's bed. The figures sit on the floor because they don't yet feel worthy of taking seats from protagonists. They draw straws using threads from the shag rug, and Violet gets the shortest. She walks to the foot of Florence's bed, takes a folded piece of paper out of her pocket and clears her throat.

"I would like to recount my experience for you all today, just to give you a taste of what it's like being inside one of Hannah's books."

Violet pauses for a second to look out at her audience.

"Question: has anyone here ever been in one of Hannah's novels? Put up your hand. Come on. Don't be shy."

"She's only written one!" grumbles Florence, like it actually affects her in some way.

"Well, were any of you in that one?"

Slowly hands go up until about half of the characters in attendance have their hands up.

"Great. About fifty percent of you. Around the figure I was expecting. And can someone tell me why they may have been subjected to such an experience?"

Mia is the first to put up her hand. "I was bad."

"Good," responds Violet. "Anyone else?"

Hilda, without putting up her hand, calls out, "Because I deserved it."

"Well said, Hilda. That's exactly the kind of response I'm looking for. Being put in a novel, especially one of Hannah's, always implies some kind of punishment." Violet pauses to look down at her notes on a podium that has just sprung out of nowhere. "Can anyone tell us more about what it feels like in there? Piranesi?"

"Very warm. I had to take my clothes off." He looks around at the others with wide knowing eyes.

"Absolutely! It can really heat up in there."

"Wet!" shouts Jorgen, wringing his hands together, which nobody has a clear picture of so that will be changed later.

"Wet. Indeed. But you haven't seen anything yet. Anyone else?"

Nobody offers a response. "Well, I'd like to give you another word to sink your teeth into," says Violet, looking more excited by the second. "Dark!"

"Oh yeah" can be heard coming from a number of the audience members. "Too true. Too true," nods Gran into her bananas and custard, which has just arrived, piping hot.

"Next time you find yourself in one of her books," says Violet, smiling, "make sure to keep in mind that it's going to be uncomfortable—wet and dark and sweaty—but that it's just a book. It's not real. It's just a story you happened to get stuck in. It will end. All books do. And you'll get your lives back. Trust me on that one. I'm living proof. I played The Girl in 2009 and I've been on vacation ever since!

"Thank you. And goodnight!"

Applause machine. Smiles all around.

Before anyone can stop her, Hilda has parked herself behind the podium.

"Thanks, Vi. I think I speak for everyone when I say that we all needed to hear that."

More applause. Petering out. Gone. Just the breath of our cast filling my mind.

"Before we move on—I know that Bill has a few things to say—I just wanted to say that, yes, I am pregnant. This is not a beer belly!" Laughter. "And that I do intend to give birth eventually—probably when none of you is looking. The baby should really come as a surprise, no?"

"How long are you going to hold on to that thing?" asks Florence, who has three of her own.

"Until the time is right. It will be right. I just don't know when. I just want you to know that there will be a birth and that it will be mine—not Violet's, not yours, Florence, but mine."

Hilda has a lot more to say—she can see Mia's shoulder touching Jorgen's, Jorgen's touching Mia's. She can see the hot flush of infidelity trespassing across her husband's cheek—but she thinks better of it. TV Drama can wait, she decides, stepping down from the stage and rushing back to her spot on Florence's bed.

Bill takes the stage next. "Thanks, Hilda."

Throat cleared, predictably. Sip of water. Sweaty night of the cabaret, the shuffling laughter of a human crowd. He lives for this.

"Evening everybody." Bill smiles out at his audience, conveniently masked by the glare of the spotlight. "We all know why we've come here this evening, but none of us is quite sure where we're going."

"Too true," mutters Jorgen.

"I'd like to put forth a theory, if I may. It's something I've been stewing over for a while now, right Hilda?"

From the end of Florence's bed, Hilda smiles broadly up at him. "He doesn't stop talking about it," she whispers to Florence, who erupts into peals (peals? really?) of laughter.

"Typically, a character only gets one shot. On occasion, there's a second novel, sometimes even a third. But readers get bored. They tire of us. They eventually seek out other psychological case studies to examine. We are simply not that interesting. Not everything is about us. The world doesn't revolve around us."

MEDITATIVE MOMENT for all of us solipsists out there. All that exists is the sound of children playing in the background, the hum of the furnace, a snow-covered neighbourhood, sun streaking on through, and icicles dripping from the gutters of my house. And that's not even the half of it. Sky. Trees. Snow clouds lifting and moving on to the next town. A street lamp waiting to go on shift. It is morning here in Canada and this is the kind of snow scene one might expect.

"SO WHAT'S YOUR POINT?" asks Violet.

"Well, do you like it when the reader tires of you? Puts your book down and turns off the light? Takes you back to the library? Or worse, doesn't even finish reading your story?"

"It's not my favourite thing, I'll admit."

"This book is different. In this one we get to be in more than one book," says Bill.

"Four, I heard," says Mia.

"Really? Four? I thought it was three," says Piranesi

"Well, it's a bunch anyway and we can kind of chop and change. Mix and match," says Bill.

"Is that such a good thing?" asks Jorgen. "I like to know where I am and what's going on."

"I don't know. I guess I was kind of excited about the thought of not being stuck in one book," says Bill. "I've never liked that, personally. I always had a hard time accepting the idea of being a set character. It's just not natural. In this book we can be ourselves. And nobody will tire of us or write descriptions of us in Fiction 101."

"And?" Violet is growing impatient with her coworker.

"And . . . Nobody will expect anything from us. We cannot be out of character because we were never in it to begin with. And we can go anywhere we want to go."

"Anywhere!?" shout the figures in unison.

"Anywhere."

"And can we be ourselves?" asks Mia.

"Yes. Completely . . . Or not."

"Or not?" Jorgen is confused.

"Or not. You can be yourselves or you can be what's written down here or you can be anything you damn well please! She doesn't own us. She's not the boss of us!"

"What about *History Book*? What about *The Archives*?" asks Piranesi. "We must respect *The Archives*."

"Meaningless."

THE CAST OF THIS NOVEL and countless others suddenly sprout new outfits. Costume Design is always the place to start. They move around the room, hooking up with the right people of the right genders. Then they look up at Bill, who is so handsome he makes the spotlight rattle.

"One more question," says Jorgen. "Are we still characters? Or are we human beings?"

"You're human beings," says Bill, almost in a whisper.

Loud applause, particularly coming from the etched palms of the field trippers, can be heard all the way to the recreation room. Dr. Grebing's field trip is over. His artists, those bright lights of the cinema, of the perfect novel, are already off—they know what's good for them—heading for a lifetime of Ferris wheel rides and candy floss tooth rot in some other book's Margate. Heading for Bestseller Fiction where they will rest their tired bodies on the shelves of airport bookstores and reveal their beauty to a boardroom of Hollywood bigwigs.

By the time the elderly residents have shuffled or wheeled themselves down the hallway to find out what is going on in Florence's room, our people have been neatly shelved within well-developed paragraphs, nestled comfortably between one unnecessary punctuation mark and the next.

Four

IT'S A TUESDAY MORNING many years before Violet becomes of the Yellow Curtains. She's something to look at if you have an imagination and can fill in the much-needed details, get past the too-many browns and navy blues, little if any makeup, the dark under-eye circles that reveal an intolerance to some unknown staple in her diet, and fingers thinning inside themselves even though she is only in her early thirties. You've got to spruce and line her features, tuck and trim her figure and pluck the tiny balls of wool that have sprung like fungi on the worn surfaces of her tights and cardigan.

She has already begun to lose her hair. The doctor has told her it is normal to lose hair during pregnancy, particularly if she has been under any stress lately? It has started to concern her a little, enough to ask her doctor about it, but she is not yet at the stage of wearing a hat and nowhere near, poor woman, the day she will walk into Selfridges to get fitted for a wig.

Violet has asked her daughter to hold onto her hand because there is traffic and it is dangerous it can squish you heaven above the thought, but she is in the "no want!" stage and refuses. Grabbing her daughter by the hand and feeling the hand slip so that she has to grip hard around the tiny wrist, Violet feels all kinds of clouds of anger balloon from her inner child.

The rain of London has been following her all morning and suddenly it buckles and rivers right down the front of Violet's skirt, turning her boots wet brown, pasting her daughter's new hair to her new skull while Violet's hair springs from its moorings, trapped spirals fuzzing up, up and away.

Their house is way too far off. They will never get there at this rate, Violet thinks, at the same time grabbing her daughter roughly and stuffing her, a rolled carpet with dangling tassels of legs, under her arm. Shopping in the other hand to balance things out, she grimaces and curses her way along some well-known London street, hating herself for not allowing her daughter to move at her own pace; hating the baby inside her, panting for iron, for the blood of some animal's liver.

The daughter, who we haven't yet been introduced to, howls at the rain and the passing buses and cars and hurrying wet pedestrians to save her. This screaming, wet eyed, wet headed snail is so beautiful.

AGAIN THE STORY COMES ONE DAY AT A TIME. Again it would be unfair to use the word story.

Madame Bovary is Elizabeth Taylor at her dressing table in a Steinbeck novel. The curtains drift into the room. The curtains are sucked tight to the window frame. Madame Bovary is a photograph of a woman on a book cover looking over her shoulder at train tracks shining with rain.

Here we are again, ducking and giggling among the billowing sheets of a costume drama. Pillows up our sweaters, flour on our hands, bloodied handkerchiefs crumpled springing from a small white hand.

I envy the trotting narrative. Stopping for no man. Pulling away from one station and into the next. And then and then and then.

AND THEN VIOLET GETS HOME. Drenched, flustered, relieved. She takes her shoes off and thro-ohws them in the lake, stokes the fire, adds some more coal, pulls let's call her Madame Bovary's winter coat and hat and scarf and gloves off and sets her in front of the fire to toast and play with her blocks and dolls. Violet goes to the kitchen, peels an orange and brings it with a cloth and a glass of water to her daughter. They eat together, pulling faces, stealing segments from between each other's teeth with little snatching bites and growls.

Violet pushes back the hair on Madame Bovary's forehead, now almost dry from the heat of the fire, and smiles at her.

"You need to listen to mummy, you know? The baby needs me to be strong and healthy and happy. When mummy asks you to do something you need to do it, OK?"

Madame Bovary isn't yet two years old but she gets the gist of the instruction. She belongs to a narrative of great distinction and has been recycled endlessly. She is fairy tale material given the chance to live a real life. The days are long and there are moments when things sag and even buckle, which makes her pine for the unexpected and the scandalous.

VIOLET AND MADAME BOVARY REMAIN AT HOME for the rest of the day. They are already eating dinner when Bill comes home from the brewery. Violet hates Bill when he first walks in at the end of the day. She spends the last few hours before his arrival praying for him to walk through the door and relieve her of her duties, but when he does she cannot stop herself from fantasizing a plate—*Bam!*—right in the centre of his forehead.

Five

CUT AND PASTE THE CROSSWORD PUZZLE SCENE HERE, the scene where Violet discovers a crossword that Bill has nearly completed with mostly wrong answers. She is appalled and decides right there and then that she has married the wrong man.

Hence the affair with Bill's adopted brother, Stephen, followed by the loss of her hair, the purchase of a wig and the smoking herself to death.

The adopted brother isn't bad. He's got the kind of body you notice on somebody else's husband that you hadn't yet realized was there. He used to box. No *Eye of the Tiger*. No frozen flank scene. But still worthy of a sly peek.

He hasn't boxed in years, but his body remembers its former shape and still edges towards it under a new Christmas jumper.

Bill can't stand him, which makes the affair that much more attractive to Violet. Stephen is aware of some tension, but has no idea how deep his brother's hatred of him runs. If he had known earlier, it may have spared him some of the guilt.

Violet isn't into sparing anyone anything at this point.

Her baby, Tom Sawyer, has arrived, in a blue flurry, in the season of snow that settles, turning The Streets of London into a playground. Madame has grown prim and strong, a woman trapped in the body of a toddler, desperate to reveal her heavy, white limb-wings, to test out the victory of her sex. Violet is too busy being a mother to remember the good times. They are there. They will find their way to the surface from time to time and burst flora and burst fauna, but this is deep purple water where nothing gets touched by direct sunlight.

THE GRAPHIC NOVELIST ON THE RADIO says that everything is true to life, especially his middle aged spread, but that the affair was added to spice up the narrative. This kind of quick thinking must be supported at every step of the way. The dull dragging feet of an average person's average day has no place here.

But real life can and often does run along the same lines as fiction. This is no joke. When it happens you know you weren't born to just play dominoes with Monsieur Bovary.

A woman is bent over, her bald head popped inside the oven like a bread roll, with the words "Don't tell your father!" written down the spine of her dress in thick black marker. You know that nobody else was there all those years ago to witness this event, so you are forced to accept it as fiction inside a book on a shelf, a book that feels drafts, fingers, other books, the wood of the shelf, the nudge of the price gun, the press of the dog ear, the heat of the tea mug, the the of the the the.

But then you almost stop breathing when you see that the woman is Violet, with her exact name and address, committing suicide. Almost.

A KITCHEN CUPBOARD IS OPENED, followed by the fridge door, and shut; the television, on commercials, leaks from the next room a packet of something crinkling open.

Bill is old now. He lives alone. Violet is long dead and her replacement (how else does one describe the widower's wife?) has gone too. He speaks softly and has kind eyes. His innocence is baffling for someone who has lived so long.

Back here in the drearily lit living room of Violet's life lives a different Bill. He is split by his astrological sign, each twin presenting itself to the world as the legitimate one. He is all those monstrous things that Violet fills her children's ears with and at the same time he is a gentle spirit with a soft voice floating strands of candy floss through the memories of his son and daughter.

There is no point trying to boil him down to the bare essentials. He is not a character. He is a man constructed of the stories he has told. Violet isn't alive to defend herself when he decides to bend a particular story in his favour. He cuts and pastes where he sees fit and always comes out noble and good, a victim of those-were-warful-times. He never initiates a fight, never causes any pain.

Bill tells the stories here. We press RECORD. We listen more to the whirr of the ancient technology than to what he is saying. It's all glory days and beautiful bric-a-brac and the loveliness of all lovely women and girls. Where was he? When did he go into her bedroom, the woman? Which woman? Which wife?

His voice is the only one in the dark room. It projects above the sound of the tape recorder, above deep pockets of silence pleading to be filled.

VIOLET THROWS HER HEAD BACK and lets out a loud "Hah!"

"He said that, did he? He would. He's got a nerve to say that. Trust him to be so self-righteous!"

STEPHEN WENT TO VIOLET on a single look exchanged at a kid's birthday party. That was all it took. They both knew it was a long time coming and when the look was exchanged over the glinting belly of a bright yellow balloon there was no doubt in either of their minds what it meant. It took over a month for them to find themselves alone together indoors, but between the birthday party and the windy spring afternoon that Stephen stepped into Violet's parlour and asked, "Are the kids asleep?" not a day passed without both of them feeling sick with anticipation.

"Yes, they just went down."

"Will they wake up?"

"They shouldn't if we're quiet."

At this they both laugh, at the same time moving into a hard embrace that feels like one is saving the other from drowning but neither is sure who is saving and who is being saved. It is a loving embrace that makes them feel good to be alive. They have found the space to love each other at long last and it will go on like this until her illness turns him away.

BILL NEVER KNEW HOW MANY TIMES Violet and Stephen made love. The day he found them together in his bed was the same day that he walked out for good. Violet had to fumble through her imagination for a story good enough to stop her daughter's incessant crying and her son's near expulsion, for getting into fights, from school. She faked her rage in the beginning, but after doing that for long enough she forgot that she'd never even been angry in the first place, only relieved. The wind had already changed direction, though, leaving her with the anger stuck to her mouth, lacquered into the grooves on her forehead.

BY THE TIME STEPHEN LEAVES VIOLET'S HOUSE it has started to rain. He has neither a hat nor an umbrella, but he walks slowly, from time to time tipping his head back to feel the rain do a music video down his face. The season is right. Sap rises to the occasion all around him as the city waits for its cue to let everyone see clearly now.

THE CHILDREN HAVE BEEN SLEEPING for much longer than usual. Violet waits in the doorway for them to wake up. It takes so long that she decides to bustle around the room accidentally on purpose. When she rustles the curtains, Madame Bovary opens her eyes.

The way she looks at her mother is terrifying. How can she know?

"Been there, done that," she says in one look.

Violet turns away from the window to see that Madame is awake and Tom has started to stir. "Hello, my little ones. Are you awake? Did you just wake up? Shh. Come, my darlings. Why don't we go out to the park? We can splash in the puddles. You can wear your new boots," and on and on like this down the stairs and into the bathroom at which point her voice gets lost behind the sound effect of running water.

Six

VIOLET IS STANDING IN THE DOORWAY OF HER KITCHEN. Stock still, eyes closed, one hand clamped over her mouth. In a sudden whoosh she sprints down the hallway and up the long narrow staircase, two, sometimes three stairs at a time. Once she reaches the second floor she throws open the bedroom door so hard that it bangs against the wall.

The lamp on Bill's bedside table is where the lamp should be. The alarm clock ticks the forlorn sound of my grandfather's teeth submerged in a plastic mug beside three Fisherman's Friends. On the table is a glass of water, perhaps sipped from once, but no more, lined with bubbles that tell us it is stale. There is a crossword puzzle cut from its newspaper and half finished. It is anchored by a pen, not a pencil. To the left and slightly below the puzzle, pointed at by the tip of the pen, is a watch. Violet snatches up the watch and shoves it into the pocket of her apron, keeping the one hand completely still, tensed beyond its usual limits and the other over her open mouth.

Bill came home last night after dark. He didn't enter the bedroom until after Violet retired at a quarter past ten. Pause. She was already asleep. Pause. Afraid to wake her, he undressed and got into bed without switching on his bedside light. In the morning, he got up before dawn and again avoided turning on the light. He could not, therefore, have seen the watch. Pause. Case closed.

Or is it? Violet did not hear Bill come in and neither did she hear him leave. A day spent with children is enough to turn anyone into a bag of bricks at the bottom of the ocean of sleep. She could not know whether Bill had turned the light on or not. If he had, he would have recognized Stephen's watch without even picking it up. It had been their father's, and on his deathbed, as a way to show his sons that he loved them equally, he gave the watch to the son most likely to feel less loved, the adopted one. Bill had coveted it ever since and at a Christmas party had even offered Stephen a grandfather clock in exchange. The morning after, slouched on the toilet with a hangover thumping behind his temples, he had felt close to tears. There was nothing he could say in sobriety that could cover up just how badly he wanted that watch to love him.

Violet tries to imagine what Bill would have done if he had seen the watch there, but she suddenly and sadly realizes that she doesn't know him well enough to be sure. She doesn't take him for a crime-of-passion sort of man, but then she has never done anything this hideous.

At this thought, Madame Bovary calls out from the next door bedroom. Violet will have no time to prepare her explanation between now and dinner when Bill will sit facing her over his steaming plate of Typical British Food. There is no time now to return the watch to Stephen. The only option Violet has is to hide it.

Quickly, perhaps too quickly, she decides on the lower tier of her sewing kit, underneath some scraps of never-to-be-used material. On selecting this hiding place, unfortunately for her, fortunately for the plot, she is unaware of one very important detail: Bill has lost a button on his favourite work shirt.

And, yes, he can sew.

And, yes, here we let out a sigh of relief because there is nothing worse than an unsolved mystery buried forever in a sewing kit that sinks with a ship in a terrible storm and is never discovered by a pod of wet-faced, treasure-thirsty divers.

Seven

JORGEN IS WORKING. The afternoon stretches out before Hilda, saggy and grey. She is living in a time before the internet, before long telephone conversations. She is not in the mood to write a letter or listen to *History Book* on the radio.

Hilda looks out the window at what winter has done to her garden—dampened everything down to the bone, making it almost impossible to even imagine summer's bare-skinned recklessness.

She will paint a picture of the garden.

She gathers all her materials: box of watercolours, two paintbrushes (the only two she has), pad of paper, pencil, glass of water, old rag and an apple (she is hungry but doesn't want the moment to pass while she prepares something to eat). She takes a pee and puts on her coat, a hat, gloves and a long scarf that she wraps around her neck so many times that she feels trapped, panicked. She loosens it, takes her materials outside, puts them on the patio and then goes back for a chair, a cushion and a blanket to put over her legs.

For a while Hilda roughly sketches what she sees in front of her. A wide, flat valley dotted with bushes and trees, demarcated by fences or low walls. At the end of her garden is a wire fence overrun with brown vines. To her right there is a large cherry tree, completely bare with no hint of the fruit to come, intersecting perfectly with the compositional grid she has inside her head. To her left is a bird bath. It ties the tree to the fence to the perfectly placed clouds. Even the birds seem to come and go as if choreographed.

AFTER A BIT Hilda sees that the scene in front of her and the grey lines on her lap have very little to do with one another. She scribbles hard across her picture and turns to a fresh sheet, one that carries the dent of her frustration in shallow grooves across the page. To these she turns.

She draws with purpose, as if she knows exactly what it is she wants to depict when in fact there is nothing inside her head at all. She sees figures have formed unintentionally and goes to them with gifts of facial features. Eyes are everywhere. Hands. Mouths are all the same—small dots of surprise. There is a purse that clicks loudly when you shut it, a tissue held out in a breeze, a needle and thread hurrying through the thigh of a woman. Leaves are everywhere, or maybe they aren't leaves at all but the idea of leaves. They have no veins, no structure, no uniformity. It is just that they fall about as leaves do, here and there with no set plan, like small flowers that decorate grass. She sees that some areas are denser, others less so; sometimes her hand has been heavy and at others so light as to leave little more than the dust from a moth's wing.

She turns to all the nooks, takes her pencil to all the crannies. More figures appear, a flock of them, sprung from where his feet pass, born of the tiny blue-jewel flowers in the grass on the school playing field, figures that must grace this world, in all their insignificance. Stick figures, some with expressions that work, others with features purged from view, slipping voiceless from the moral hands that grace the polished banisters of money. Malnutrition. Poverty. Without colour, without light, they rise. Up the page, darkening the horizon with their body politic, with their mouthfuls of so much to say.

Excited now, surprised by what has come out of her, Hilda turns the pad and looks at it from every angle—portrait, upside down landscape, upside down portrait. She wants to put the picture here. Let it speak for itself. The pleasure of concentration has taken her to that place where even her madness can run free, free of lobotomy, free of electroshock therapy, down to the bottom of the hospital pool with the sudden coolness of water on her side.

HILDA REALIZES SHE IS FREEZING. She gathers up her supplies and hurries back into the house. When she gets inside she checks the clock. Two hours have passed. She closes the pad of paper and slides it under a cushion on the hallway bench. There is something obscene about her picture that she feels she must hide.

Her fingertips are silver and this pleases her. Without washing them she goes up to the bedroom, slides under the heavy blankets and closes her eyes. She stays in this position, listening to her empty stomach growling until she hears Jorgen fumbling around in the darkening kitchen below.

Eight

THE HOUSE IS DARK. Jorgen thinks that Hilda must be out. She makes him jump when she steps out of the blackness of the hallway into the lighted kitchen. She looks drowsy, has her cardigan kimono-wrapped tightly around her chest.

"Where have you been?"

"At a group meeting."

"What's the deal with this sect, Jorgen?"

He glares at her. "It's not a sect."

"Is it a Christian sect?"

"It's not a sect, but, yes, we do consider ourselves Christian."

"What's the basic premise? Is there a holy book?"

"The Bible."

"So you are Christians."

"I just said that."

"Since when were you a Christian?"

"I've always been a Christian." Jorgen stops for a moment. "Have I?"

"It's news to me," says Hilda, "but we've got to say something and this is what is coming out. I'll just continue, OK?"

"Fair enough. I'll just say that Christian bit again, yeah?" Pause. "I've always been a Christian."

"Since when? We didn't even get married in a church."

"I lapsed for a while."

"A while? What, like twenty years?"

"A lot of Christians stray temporarily, but then they come back, especially as they age."

"Fuck that. I'm not coming back."

Jorgen frowns. Shakes his head. He turns to the table to pour himself some tea from an empty teapot. He makes the sound of liquid pouring into a cup. Terribly done. She waits for the slurp. It's better, but still not that good.

"What's the matter?" she asks, a little annoyed that he's broken her rhythm.

"You wouldn't say the word 'fuck.' It's not your style."

"You're probably right. OK. I'll try 'screw' instead."

"Screw that!" she says, raising her voice. "*I'm* not coming back."

"I like the italics on 'I'm,'" he says. "Works well. But I don't think you'd say 'screw' either."

"What would I say?"

"I don't know. I'm not the writer."

JORGEN HAS BEEN A DEVOTEE of the Back to Life movement for over a month. With Mia, the conversion was easy. The two of them adapted quickly to the diet, felt themselves levitate to the music, the singing, the twirling ecstasy that left their shyness by the wayside and made them animal. Everybody loving everybody. Everybody part of one big family.

"WHAT DO THEY SAY ABOUT ME?" asks Hilda, almost slyly, like she's digging for evidence of a crime.

"They'd like it if you joined us."

"Well, you can tell them from me that religion is the opiate of the masses."

"Did you make that up?"

"Of course I made it up! And it's true."

"So what?" He ignores her. Turns away.

"Screw you and your cult."

"Thank you," he says, turning to the kitchen sink and pretending to wash dishes.

Jorgen's back starts to shake. Weak with the silliness of dialogue on a page, flagrantly ousting the stumbling *ums* and *urs* of real communication, Jorgen cannot stop laughing. This sets Hilda off. Delighted, they lean on each other, happy to be close because they've always liked each other and hoped that this would be the book that would bring them together at last.

Hilda. Calm now: "And screw Mia! The two of you are like a pair of children."

"At least somebody around here is a child." They lose it again. Laugh so hard that they start to cry. They have lost it so many times today that everybody around them is starting to get annoyed.

"That was a low blow."

"Well, at least somebody around here is blowing somebody."

"And another."

"I will keep them coming until the great Lord of my loins comes down from your high horse," says Jorgen, wiping the tears from his cheeks.

"He's not coming."

"You wait. He is."

Hilda is adamant, adamantine, granite in her sturdy set of beliefs that defy the gravity of faith. Oh how it pushes against the chest like a slab of concrete! She is well aware of the scientific logic swelling out along the orderly rows of pews, depressing the tongue of the gagging child. "Pour it straight down the throat!" shout the believers. "We cannot afford to spill one drop of the cherished elixir from the little bastard's mouth!"

"In your dreams, Jorgen. In your dreams," Hilda spits from her laughing-wide mouth, her crumbling faith in her body thrown at Jorgen like a quiet tea towel.

Tale of the Small Green Weeds

I

IN ROME, I FOUND MY CALLING: the skirting of ruins in synthetic fabrics.

What did my MEC bag contain? Everything I ever needed. Lip salve, Euros, a roll of 200 speed colour film, a ripped plastic baggie of Turkish apricots, a pen with no lid, a bottle of water, and a postcard of Caius Cestius' pyramid.

PIRANESI'S ETCHINGS SHOULDER THE HORROR of pestilence, lean the lame and destitute against the architectural masterpiece that is Ancient Rome. I want to know if he is for the safe injection site or against it; if he is cleaning the streets or sending the streets to the dogs.

Tourists charge at his commissions with their guide books flapping. His pyramid postcard attracts the Romantic Era to hover forever and amen over the Non-Catholic Cemetery, summer traffic choking back the symphony of his lines.

Cestius' pyramid is not a crumbling bombed-out monument looted by the mob of discontent. It remains, trying to decide where it wants to be, at one with the past, not so sure about the present or about the dead piling up around it, married unwillingly to Rome's caustic exhaust.

When the tomb is opened, all that wheezes out is a draft.

Nine

"DOCTOR? IS THIS YOURS?" Hilda leans around the office door, arm outstretched with the doctor's silver watch hanging from it. It has a good weight. She thinks of her father misplacing his watch in different rooms around the house and her mother invariably telling him exactly where to find it without even looking up from her work.

"Oh, yes. Thank you. Hilda, isn't it?"

"Yes, Doctor." Hilda lowers her eyes as he takes the watch from her hand. The brush of his fingers is deliberate.

"Listen. There's an art collection project I'm currently in charge of and I need an assistant. Know anything about art?"

"What kind of art?"

"Art. Painting. Drawing."

She wants to tell him about her drawings. They frighten her with their madness. To look at one is to hold a mirror up to her unconscious.

"No, not really. No more than the average person."

"Well, do you like art?" Maybe he is taking the wrong angle. Dr. Grebing doesn't care if she paints or draws. He doesn't even care if she has ever looked at a piece of art in her life. He likes her red hair. He likes her wide hips. That uniform looks better on her than it does on any other nurse in the hospital.

"I suppose so."

This is enough of a cue for the doctor. "Good then. I'm transferring you to the project. You start tomorrow. 9 a.m."

"I'm on nights."

"Not any more. You can go home after medications. Another nurse will take your shift. Goodnight, Hilda."

"Goodnight, Doctor." Night doctor. In darkness. Complicit.

She stops hugging the door jam and goes off to administer medication to the ten women on the ward. Pills stick to their lips, catch on the way down, spill from a shaky hand shaky cup, poor love. Hilda hardly notices. She is not prepared to be courted. It would distract her from the full time job she has of keeping tabs on her husband.

BY 7:30 HILDA IS ON HER BICYCLE being German and beautiful. Up close you could list the flaws. Crows have landed where she has smiled too hard for too many years. Cellulite dimples the underside of her thighs, but only for her husband's eyes. Her hips will never let her forget that they are there. But from here, in this tree, looking down at our passing damsel we see flames of dyed red hair catching all the highlights this song has on offer.

She shoots down the darkening lane, a flash through the leaves—our red heroine on her way home.

Jorgen and Mia are in the front room. They hear "bicycle wheels on gravel"—a personal favourite.

"Shit!"

Trousers and legs and flushed cheeks and doors closing and hair straighter straighter straighter and tucked behind the ears, and blouse tucked into the nylons that may or may not have been invented, that would never have even been worn by a woman so young and so bohemian straightening the room and the world and the lies that have not yet been thought up with her cousin's one and only love-husband.

There is no mail in the mail box but Hilda rummages around in there for as long as she can, clicking her fingernails and rings against the metal. She is a mother giving her children enough time to hide. She can hear their hearts booming in their mouths. When she enters the living room her nostrils exchange the undeniable smell of cum for the smell of the flowering trees in their lane.

"I got off early."

Jorgen looks up from his paper, opened onto a convincing page—Sports—and says, "Oh, that's great. Hi."

What a lovely "Hi." My love, my darling, say it again, say it in my ear, say it between my legs, say it because you've been away at sea and I am your sailor-woman.

"Hi Hilda. How come you're home?" Kicking herself for asking such a dead-give-away question, Mia comes into the room all fey and curious wearing a sweater that is way too big for her because she wants her hands to be nowhere to be seen.

"I have a new job. It starts tomorrow, so I got out of my night shift."

"What is it?" asks Jorgen, forgetting for a moment that he is weak and on the verge of tears while at the same time melting at the core of his torso a throbbing sexual bliss.

"Assistant art collector."

Hilda shrugs and leaves the room, her cardigan shimmering off her shoulders into wings struggling against glass.

Ten

BILL OPENS THE DOOR TO FIND HILDA standing there,wet from a rain storm. She looks at him from under her dark eyebrows, waiting for him to invite her in. He doesn't. He is thinking that he should have met her when he was twenty and slim.

She pushes past him, pulling her coat off while navigating the narrow hallway made narrower by a hat stand, shoe rack and hall table overloaded with worthless bric-a-brac that Bill believes will be worth a fortune one day.

"How do you do it, Bill? How do you stand being who you are?" She is sitting on the armchair closest to the door, half on, half off, as if she hasn't decided whether to stay or not.

He is silent. He's had this conversation with Hilda before and is getting tired of it. He can never give her a good answer.

"In this novel I'm supposed to do two things that I'd never do in real life. One," she presses one thumb down with the other. "I'm supposed to act like I don't care what Jorgen is up to. And two," she pushes down her index finger with the same reliable thumb. "I'm supposed to throw myself in front of a train or some other fast moving vehicle in a fit of torment and despair.

"Do I look like the kind of woman that would do either!?"

As usual, she is raising her voice. Bill is uncomfortable because the nosy woman next door will undoubtedly corner him when he is taking out the rubbish and press him to tell her things he doesn't want to. He knows this book is on shaky ground right now, liable to be left unfinished if he doesn't do something monstrous or brave or at least romantic.

"Do you want a cup of tea?"

"No!" snaps Hilda. Then, after a short pause, "Oh, alright then. Two sugars."

Bill goes into the kitchen and they begin their conversation through the sounds of tea preparation, which helps Bill to relax.

"What did he do now?" Bill calls out, regretting it immediately.

"The usual. He's with her again. I may as well go back to first draft and start over."

"I would if I could," Bill says, under his breath.

"What?"

"Nothing. Two sugars, right?"

"Right. What? Tell me what you just said."

He enters the room carrying two piping hot cups of tea.

"Did I give that enough time?"

"Who cares!" shouts Hilda. "Nobody cares how many minutes it takes to make a cup of tea realistically. Tell me what you just said."

"God, Hilda. Let it go will you. I'm not in the mood for this today."

"You never are. You never ever have time for me. Just like everyone else." She buries her face in her hands and tries to cry but only two unconvincing whimpers come out. "I can't even cry."

"Maybe you're trying too hard, Hilda. This is less complicated than you're making it out to be. Just be yourself."

"What about you? Did you really choose to be that thick? Some of the things that come out of your mouth, Bill. They make me wonder if she dropped you on your head."

They laugh and sip tea.

"I like this room. It's cozy. You've made it nice in here, haven't you? Do you ever get lonely?"

"All the time."

"What do you do about it?"

"I do the crossword."

They laugh again.

"Fucking crossword scene!" says Hilda. "As if we haven't read that enough times. It should have been cut years ago."

"But don't you like the bit when I think that the Taj Mahal is in China?"

"Ha! Yeah. That's so thick. Aren't you pissed off?"

"Nah. I chose that line."

"Some choice."

He gets up and goes over to the window. It's raining hard and already dark. The light from the streetlamp outside, Bill's very own street lamp, turns the raindrops on the window orange. He opens the window a fraction and turns to look at Hilda.

"This story hasn't even been written yet. Your story, yes. But that's been and gone and it didn't even get good reviews. This story is the one that matters. You'll figure out who you are and when you do you'll tell me over a cup of tea that I make so quickly that even the most unobserving reader will notice. That'll be our trademark, our thing."

She is sitting deep in the armchair now, thrilled at the cold air coming in and the sound of rain on the glass.

"What's for supper?" she says, noticeably cheered up.

Eleven

DAYS HAVE GONE BY UNHAD. Violet isn't sure how many. She knows it is Friday because this morning, standing like sentries guarding her doorstep, there were two pints of milk instead of one.

Tom is asleep in his crib and has been for over an hour. Madame is playing quietly with her dolls. The hour has been one great gulp of snow air. Violet has had two cups of tea, clipped her nails, put lotion on her face and legs and hands, and stared out the window at the rain. Her mind is filled with thoughts that anger her with their mediocrity. Sometimes she stops to consider the conversation shunting softly through her head: How is Tom? Still at the boob. He's biting, you know. And Madame? Oh, she's been very sick. Poor thing. Her temperature went down this morning, but she's still very needy. Oh, Vi. I totally understand. My Rachel was sick like that when she was a baby and it was so hard. It's Friday. I don't know what I want to eat. What will Bill want? I'm sick of food. I don't like anything. It's all boring. I think that's it. I'm bored. Totally and completely bored. I didn't check the post. Maybe I'll wait until Madame wakes up. She likes to check the post.

And on and on like this until night comes and she gets knocked out by sleep.

She needs a project, a plan of action, something to be passionate about. But what? And it's not like there is time to do anything anyway. Everything gets interrupted. Half the fish breaded, half a soak in the tub, half a sandwich, half a cup of tea, half a phone call, halfway through the washing-up. So always in the back of her mind is this something or other that needs to be done, but it loses its pleasure or its momentum by the time she returns to it and besides by then there is already something else to half do and the thought of that something else leaves no room in Violet's head for French theorists to bury their tiny hatchets.

The hour starts to gape into two hours. So much of the day is spent praying for some time alone, but then once it arrives it spills out all over the place and all she wants to do is tidy it up and get back to the job of being a mother. The time swells fat from the clock, calls to her, taunts her, asks her what she is going to do now that she has what she wants. Her nails are trimmed, her skin is smooth, the rain has stopped. The street outside is busy with people's ambition. They move in particular directions for particular reasons, rather than circling the block or the park as Violet does, always with the pram before her like a statement.

"WHEN I'M CONFINED AT HOME, going outside becomes a luxury. When I take the bin out, especially at night, I go loopy for that cold, fall air. I actually huff it. It takes all of me not to take my clothes off and roll in the grass. It's not like that would be pleasurable in any way. There isn't even much grass, not enough to do a full roll, only perhaps half of one. It's just that it would wash away this feeling of being stuffed up inside a roll of left-over carpet with the radiator blaring away and Tom picking threads out of the rug and eating them. They come out in his poo and I always think I'll stop him next time he does it, but when the next time comes he's down there on the floor, concentrating so hard on his little task—one thread, into the mouth, two threads, into the mouth. I can't bring myself to stop him. It's just wool.

"But sometimes it's so boring sitting there watching him eating the threads, listening to Madame shuffling a crayon over a colouring book, feeling drugged and dull because the house is too hot but I'm too lazy to get up and open a window. And hours go by cooped up inside like this so that when I have to go outside, usually to take the bin out, it's like I'm on vacation. I look up at the night sky and imagine I'm out on the moors with my hair twisting about in the wind. Mist on my face, gloomy hills in every direction, not a person or a car or a bus . . ."

"Who said you could have a monologue?" Bill has just come in from work.

"Nobody," says Violet.

"You might want to let the others know. They might want one too."

"I'm not stopping them."

"You kind of are. If we all started doing monologues, it would be a bit chaotic. Never mind the waste of paper."

"Well, there was nobody to talk to."

Bill is already opening the newspaper. He reads both *The Sun* and the *Daily Mirror* religiously. On Saturdays and Sundays he sometimes prides himself on the fact that he reads every single bit of text in both newspapers, even the advertisements.

Violet thinks it's a total waste of his time. They could do so much more if he didn't spend his time reading newspapers.

Earlier on that day she had taken a look at one of his half finished crosswords. Noticing an error—in pen—she had gone back over each of his clues to find out where he'd gone wrong.

At dinner, unable to eat because she is nursing Tom, feeling in the mood for a fight, she asks him: "Do you know where the Taj Mahal is?"

"The what?"

"The Taj Mahal." This time Violet says it long and slippery.

"China? Sounds Chinese. Pass me the vinegar, love."

"No. It's in India. Did you seriously not know that?"

"Why should I know where the Trage Mahel is? What's so important about it, anyway?"

Violet is looking at her husband of six years in disbelief.

She watches him chew grossly on his fried fish. A little of the juice is dribbling from the corner of his mouth, down his chin, a greasy wet rivulet of fish juice. It repulses her. He is fat from eating too much meat, drinking too much beer. He smiles at her, revealing a bit of food stuck in his teeth. She'd rather look at Madame's face, even though it is smeared with mashed potatoes, her hair gelled up into little peaks like the top of a shepherd's pie.

"What's the matter with you?" Bill asks. "Any more fish?"

Violet, too disturbed to answer him, shifts Tom to the other breast.

"Did you go to school?" she asks.

"Me? Of course I did. Went to Saint Martin's Primary School. Good school that was. There were some very nice teachers there."

Very nice. He always said *very nice*. Everyone was very nice. At least women were. Men were *alright* or *not bad*. He didn't have much of a vocabulary, really, but she'd never really thought about it.

"Oh, you like the fish then, do you?"

"Oh, yes, it's very nice."

"I got it from Jack down the market."

"He's not bad, but I prefer going to Maureen for fish."

"She's nice, isn't she?"

"Oh, yes, very nice. Stellar woman."

Stellar was another of his favourites, a word that makes Violet's skin crawl. A heavy wave of nausea comes over her. She lights a cigarette, watches the rain muttering against the window, the streetlight spilling its golden cargo into the kitchen. She is calmed by the sight. It makes her think of black earth under moonlight. Her uncle's farm where she and her brothers tried to walk in the deep mud but fell in their boots like flower heads on broken stems. She thinks about the times in her life before she met Bill when she would have conversations with her friends in the pub about the meaning of life and the significance of dreams or about why people did the things they did.

"Where's that fish then?"

Tom looks up from his mother's breast, his lips wet with milk.

A sudden rage expands in Violet's throat. It wants to burst her pipes wide open with shouting. She smacks the *Mirror* up and out of Bill's hands. He is left with a confused look on his face and chunks of newspaper sticking out of his fists.

"Hang on a minute, Vi. Wait!"

"What?" Violet is smiling.

"I wouldn't be eating and reading the paper at the same time. You have to choose one or the other."

"I know, but we had the *Bam!* plate thing earlier. So just as I was about to smash my fist down on your dinner, I had second thoughts and came crashing down into that gorgeous sound of ripping paper. Better, don't you think? An infinitely more satisfying sound effect."

"Probably. But just so you know, there's a time for plate smashing and a time for newspaper slapping. And I just have to say it because if I don't, who will? Who on earth doesn't know where the fucking Taj Mahal is?"

Violet laughs in Bill's face. "You! Apparently."

"Just get me some more fish, woman!" Bill smiles and holds his palm against Violet's cheek in pure loving tenderness snapped right from the apex of a stage play.

"Aye, aye, captain!" she shouts, handing Tom to his father and taking a potato-pasted Madame from her highchair just to throw her up—whee!—right at the moon of the ceiling with all those stars ripening around it.

Twelve

FLORENCE HAS THREE CHILDREN. She loves her children well by playing with them even when she doesn't feel like it. They want to be around her, to snuggle up to her when she is talking to a neighbour in the doorway, to run to her and jump into her arms when she is walking to meet them, Stephen coming up behind them slowly, looking almost shy at Florence's pretty, smiling face, her coming forth.

FLORENCE AND STEPHEN are in separate rooms of the house. Between them is a wave of fear and suspicion that sloshes against the walls closest to them. They feel the flood coming. Stephen sips from an amber-coloured bottle that he first cleaned carefully with water and soap, stoppering the hole with his thumb while he shook the corners clean of cough syrup. The bottle contains gin that comes from a larger bottle safely stashed at the bottom of a box of baby clothes. He is shaky for the right dose. The children are out in the street throwing snowballs. One hits the window, startling him from his task. The thumping in his chest thickens.

Florence has tidied the house enough already. Snow is falling again. The children will be cold when they get home. She calls to Stephen, knowing exactly where he is and what he is doing but pretending to herself that she doesn't.

"Can you start a fire?"

He enters the room suspiciously quickly, smiling with his mouth only.

"Sure."

He picks up the coal scuttle and goes out the back to get more coal from the shed.

While he is making the fire, the children come in from the snowy street. They are fighting because I haven't given them names and so the neighbourhood kids have taken it upon themselves to name them. They are all named after swear-words. They have been crying all over the snow, melting it. The three little kittens' hands are red hot with cold. Their father is taking his sweet time to get the fire going, wanting to sweep away all of the ashes before he begins, humming through the gin light that guides him up and over the houses of London into some past utopia that was child-free and made of night-time and electric light. His bottle waits for him in the next room, but not patiently. It calls to him persistently, all day, even late at night when he has brushed his teeth and is pulling on his pajamas. Tired, but so weak when it calls his name, he tells Florence, "Just going to pop down and check that I locked the front door. Not sure if I did."

She seethes under the covers, the hard sorrow in her throat worse than the crying that won't come.

Today, though, Florence is not her usual nightingale self. She knows where the money they don't have has been going. Not caring that the kids are cold and hungry, that they will witness her rage as she witnessed her own mother's, she rushes at Stephen, grabs his face and squeezes his cheeks together so that his lips push out a kiss. Poking her nose at his mouth she breathes deeply as he pushes her back hard so that she crashes quietly into the soft stunt double space of the sofa.

Again. This time in slow motion. The kids raise their arms, their voices, run leisurely against the fug of technology towards their mother, grab onto her body and smother her with cushions, their coats, their three little kitten mittens and scarves. You've found your mittens, you wonderful kittens!

"You smell like a brewery!" she screams. "It's 10 o'clock in the morning. What are you doing? What are you doing!?"

He smashes his fist against the mantelpiece and then turns away from all of them crying on the couch and leaves the room. Florence can hear him through the wall, rummaging. "That's right!" she shouts through the house. "Don't forget your precious bottle!" She can hear the slam of the front door. She can hear the rush of falling coal into the hearth as her daughter establishes the living hum of normalcy in the room.

"I'm cold, mum. Let's get the fire going."

Florence goes into the kitchen and shuts the door. This is Bill's kitchen, she thinks. Can't they get a new fucking set?

Tale of the Small Green Weeds

II

ROME IS A CITY UPON ANOTHER CITY upon another city. Its residents and visitors live in the gap between the one hand and the other, homesick for muscle and brutality—the gatekeepers of tight and shiny lines.

The stones that once fit together, snug sliding parcels of masculinity, long to separate and plop down onto a pile of like-minded deserters. Its buildings shift back into their blueprints, making space for flora to grow there, up, like the stones, to the gods, to the light.

The postcards creep their black and white greenery. Vines devour temples just to make homes for their friends—the insects, the birds—and foliage nests its hairy victory high above a gathering of addicts and schizophrenics, crowning the fist with a mitten.

People have to go on living. The mess they make. Of their lives. Of the streets. Of their kids. They are everywhere. They can't get out of the shadows or the lines or the creases or the leaves. All those leaves to stuff them under, but they come creeping back out, under the ivy, under the hedges and the bridges and the roads. Tendrils erupt and pull at the tiles of a masterpiece, dig into the walls and slowly come to power.

PIRANESI PUTS WOMAN WITH BABE IN ARMS on the steps of the crumbling Pantheon. A Christian prop. The father is nowhere to be seen. The shadows are filled with the flotsam and jetsam of history's swooshing march forward. There is so much to fear in this black and white scratched landscape. Fruit does not hang from the trees and bushes. These man-made extravagances feed nothing but egos and wallets.

An idle man reclines on every page of Mia's coffee table art book, caught in the act of some fantasy of shelter and food. How dare he! Most are marked by sticks to set them out from all the reasonable lines. They pick among the wreckage, salvaging materials to build with, while overhead vines heave-ho the glory to the ground.

THE PEOPLE MUST EAT, must feed each other, must sleep in dry beds that do not itch, must take their clothes off and clean their bodies and dry their bodies with clean towels and put fresh clothes on and brush their hair and their teeth. The people must eat.

The people grab their sticks and pose, dwarfed by grandeur, placed at strategic spots in the compositional field to be spotted, like Waldos.

Thirteen

THE ITALIAN SAGA IS SWOON CENTRAL. Mia swaggers down its spine. Flapper girl, web cam stripper, smoking in the fug of her girlish tattoos. Her paintings-turned-social media posts make up for the grey of the world, take up whole corners of the studio of my computer in their fine brightness.

Today she has cut the length out of her dress and added it to her hair. Her bangs have been cut by a hairdresser who calls the style "Canadian high school." She used to use the British word *fringe,* like her head was a suede jacket, but *bangs* goes with "banging her," "gang bang," "head banger," and "banged up"—all of which sound heavy enough to suit Mia's new attitude.

Today she is communing with the little people in a Piranesi etching, forgetting entirely about the crumbling buildings they are meant to enlighten. Her eyes move from the buildings to the tiny figures in the foreground. She leans in closer, wishing she had a magnifying glass, wondering if any of her friends from *The Italian Saga* have shown up.

"WHERE DOES THE EYE GO FIRST?" the Art teacher asks, all loopy with pedagogical glee. Mia wants to say, "To the losers rummaging in the foreground," but worries that will be the wrong answer. "Anyone? Anyone?" squeaks the demented failed artist at the front of the class until she cannot bear it any longer and answers her own question: "To the losers rummaging in the foreground, of course!"

Mia kicks herself.

SHE HAS BEEN TO ROME AND SHE KNOWS PIRANESI. She modeled in miniature for him. He slapped her once and she liked it. How her cheek blushed with his royal blow. She wore it home for all the lusting Italian men to envy. They whistled at that slap mark. They followed it with their married eyes. They blew kisses at it. She was an advertisement for something coy, feminine, essential, torn from a magazine and found wrong in the hands of a young, impressionable girl. "They will gang-bang her!" shouts the girl's mother under the sound of a hair-dryer. "You mark my word for it!"

Mia misses the warm Rome streets. Riding bareback past the Colosseum with her feet looking for stirrups where there are none to be found. Floating through the no-nonsense; slicing through the red tape; letting the tourists do it their slow, OCD way, while she is waved on like a character in a book.

She misses lounging in the arms of a tourist, hell bent on getting her picture taken so that she can star in yet another European Tour photo album. "So dull, these creatures," she thinks, as she cuts across their predictable paths on her steed.

MIA HAS THE KIND OF BOYFRIEND that gets sloughed off to make room for life to be lived. She is the kind of girlfriend a boy cages in his fantasies, tied up, barely, after a scuffle that makes the bloodthirsty crowd wonder who is the boss of who.

The boyfriend's face appears at the classroom window. Jorgen? Mia stares back, grinning, until the bell rings and she can run to the door, hiding her grin in the flustering rush of her duffle coat and art satchel and cigarette pack opening up.

"You done?" he asks.

"Yeah. You?"

"No. But I'm taking you home anyway." He is trying to scoop her up, but she is all gear with no handles.

"Get off!" She is running and he is stooping to pick up everything she has dropped. Her mitten. Her textbook. Her satchel. Her coat. Her dress. Her shoes. Her skin. Her legs. Her eyes. Her hair. Her breasts. Her breath. Her mouth.

She comes back together once they are back at her house, warm against each other in her bed on the floor: a single mattress with two cigarette burns on the underside and the same quilt cover she had on her bed when she was ten. Her first orgasm is heard by only one of the three roommates in the house. Her second is heard by all three. His is a series of grunts that bury themselves in her hair.

Afterwards he pants in the dry grass, fingers inside her, toes touching hers, his hip and inner thighs damp with cum on hers.

THERE ARE PLACES WHERE MIA FINDS she can breathe again and they are not in *The Italian Saga*. Out from under the elbows of her mother's voice she feels the countryside spread out beneath her man like a fucking-table.

Jorgen?

Fourteen

FLORENCE COMES AT VIOLET WITH TEA full of questions. Stale ginger cake. Violet can feel the cilia in her intestines pricking a warning. Why invite her here? This woman that has taken Florence's man right out from under her, magician's cape forced out on a choreographed wind.

Florence knows that Violet knows that Florence knows what Violet has done. The truth binds them together despite the natural inclination to fall apart. Florence has wound threads around any object she can—table leg, lamp, sofa leg, fire grate, door handle—and pulled them taut around her waist where she stands in perpetual service to her sister-in-law.

Tom Sawyer is sleeping in the bed of Violet's arm, sucking blissfully.

"You'll spoil him, you know."

"Maybe."

"When are you planning on weaning him?"

"Not sure."

Violet has stopped caring what Florence thinks of her. She works hard to be everything that Flo isn't: a mistress (on certain grey afternoons) and a cruel and neglectful mother (at certain times of the month). This will all change in time—the two women might even find themselves reversed—but for now, having Stephen press her to the wall while Florence calls out inanities from the kitchen (place of all calling words) is enough of a thrill to get her over the hump of one dull week and into the next.

"I got the cake at Davidson's."

"Nice."

"On sale."

"Oh."

"Way cheaper than the corner store."

Violet lets out a massive, overdramatic sigh.

"What?"

"Just stop it, Florence. Stop this."

Florence looks out at the flimsy spokes radiating from her body. This is her doing—this intricate MoMA installation that suggests she is a shrink-wrapped fly at the centre of a web.

"I wouldn't sleep with Stephen if you paid me," says Violet, placing her plate of half-eaten cake on the floor. "I haven't slept with him."

"But *History Book* says otherwise." Ripping the threads from her claustrophobic performance piece, Florence goes over to the bookcase and takes the book down.

"Here," she says, voice rising. "Here! There's a conversation between Bill and his granddaughter." She reads: "'I came home and found them in bed together.' 'Oh God.' (That's the granddaughter speaking.) And . . . 'Then I left. I didn't see your father again until he was a grown man.' It's right here, Violet."

"Yeah. Sure. Bill's word against mine."

"Really, Violet? Really? You think I'm just going to go along with whatever you say and sweep all the egg shells up and just wind these threads back up and throw them in the sewing kit? Do you think?"

"Yes. Why not? It's Bill's word against mine. Who do you want to believe?"

"Bill."

"And Hollywood."

"Yes! Bill *and* Hollywood *and* Bestseller Fiction *and* TV Drama."

"TV Drama? You'll be adding Soap Opera next."

"*And* Soap Opera!" Florence is shouting now. "And *fucking* Soap Opera! Why not? I wouldn't put it past you, Violet. In all the written records this novel has access to, you're a chain smoking, lying whore!" Florence stops. She's wondering why Tom hasn't woken up. She leans in closer to find that Violet is using the plastic baby.

"You'd stick anything on your tit, wouldn't you?"

"Why do you care? Your kids don't even have names. And as for Stephen, it's not as if he's your *real* husband. Sometimes he even doubles as mine or Hilda's. I saw him sitting on a park bench the other day when we were doing a scene in Rome. He was Italian, for god's sake! And I swear it was him in here putting *History Book* on the shelf for you. If your windows weren't so bloody clean I wouldn't have to see so much."

"Well, if yours weren't so dirty we wouldn't be having this conversation. I'd have seen the light."

"Poetic. Look," says Violet, winding down. "We need to stop talking to one another like this. It's counterproductive. They're bringing in the PoMo sniffer dogs as we speak. They'll shut us down in the name of banning experimentation for experimentation's sake and we'll go right back to 'the-wind-tousled-his-hair' or, god forbid, 'the-sun-peeked-out-from-behind-a-cloud.' We must remain calm, Florence. Just keep talking as if nothing has happened. If you want real life, you have to play it cool. That weird thread installation, the stale cake, all of history contained in a single book—these are all things that don't happen."

"Stale cake happens."

"No. It doesn't. A person cannot time the staleness of a cake as a form of revenge. It's too perfect."

"Perhaps. But I think you're lying. I *know* you're lying. That's the whole point. In real life, these shitty and dramatic things *do* happen. They're the very fabric of The Family Secret and they end up channeled into fiction because they're safer there."

Easier to touch. Less red hot pokeresque.

At arm's length, the absurdity of a tragedy lies in small print. A death on the first page. A death on the last page. The dying cries of the murdered lover shrinking along with the print, slowly becoming fine fiction.

"YOU'LL NEVER GUESS WHAT STEPHEN SAID the other night."

"Are we back?"

"Yes. Just make it up."

"What?"

"Wow! Your dialogue is so original." Florence is laughing, mocking.

"Well, you always begin with a question."

"Well, you always begin with a 'well.' Who begins with a 'well' in real life?"

"Lots of people."

"Where have you been doing your research?"

"All over London. In all the boroughs. In all the mews and closes and rows. Around all the roundabouts."

"Oh please!"

"Just start again," Violet says impatiently.

"You'll never guess what Stephen said the other night."

"What?"

"That he wishes he could paint."

"Houses or pictures?"

"Pictures of houses. Houses full of pictures. Chimneys on fire with paint. Pictures of the two of us bound up in thread and cake and the morning light that shafts through my clean windows. Tom sleeping like a fat kitten against the pins and needles in your arm. All of this. This whole row of drama and tragedy."

Well, why doesn't he then? thinks Violet, with extra emphasis, inside her head, on the *well*.

Florence matronly slurps her cold tea and looks at the clock.

"I'd better get down to the shops before it starts to rain. This novel is heavy on the rain, huh?"

Violet sees that Tom Sawyer is waking up. She shifts him to the other breast.

"I'll just top him off and then I'll be off."

"Take your time," calls Florence, already in the kitchen where all calling must originate. She is giving Violet the finger from both hands, tongue out, making a quick grab or two for her crotch, crosseyed for a moment, some anthropological case study of The Housewife.

A neighbour observes Florence through her commercial-clean kitchen window, and guesses that Violet must be in the front room.

Fifteen

NOT LONG INTO HER AFFAIR, Violet miscarries a Romantic long poem. It trickles into the toilet—runoff from a heather-clad Scottish peak. It is only eight weeks old. Nobody will ever see its face or hold its not yet hazelnut-sized hand. She has never been this sad and, even though she cannot know it at the time, she will never be this sad again. Not when Bill leaves. Not when Stephen leaves. Not when her mother and father die on the same day in the same fire, spat from their tenth floor flat like hot nails.

The baby is Stephen's. There is no doubt, but you can never be too sure, unless you get on one of those talks shows where they do a DNA test for free.

She loves the baby immediately, loves it all the more because she isn't supposed to. The ones that come too early, half period, half person, the haunting ones, the ones that never do anything wrong, that never hurt flies or kick dogs or cry down the night. She dreams up blissful scenarios involving Stephen defending her from Bill's accusations that she has slept with half of London, then taking her to Paris to live out the rest of their days, Madame Bovary fitting in swimmingly with the locals and translating for them in restaurants and shops.

She carefully plots ways to keep the baby. She will go away in her second trimester to live in the countryside and then leave the baby with the wet nurse from first draft until she can steal away with Stephen to collect their darling child. She schemes constantly, so much so that she neglects the small things that matter and keep other people—her children and her husband—alive and not suspicious. Food isn't shopped for, let alone chopped, cooked and put onto plates. Clothes go unwashed. Mice start to take over the house, finding it easier than any other house in the neighbourhood to find food. Bill notices, but says nothing. He knows that whatever he says, it will lead to the reason his brother's watch was in the sewing kit.

THE FIRST BLOOD WAS ROUTINE. She spotted when she was pregnant with both Tom and Madame so thought nothing of it until the following evening when the cramps started. They started while she was lying in bed reading. Bill was beside her. She grimaced with the pain, letting *Madame Bovary* fall from the bed. Bill turned to her, put his arms around her and said, "What's wrong, love?" She remained silent, teeth grit against the pain.

"Nothing. Probably something I ate."

Hope rocketed inside her until more pain—harder, sharper, bent on expelling the child—sent her rushing to the bathroom. She shut herself in, not coming out until the early hours of the morning.

Bill would have been alarmed, would have pounded on the bathroom door, demanding that she come out and tell him what was wrong, if he hadn't fallen asleep. He was the kind of person who could fall asleep on a ten-minute bus ride. He planned to wait for her to return from the bathroom, but sleep overcame him and when she at last came back to bed she found him spread-eagled on her side, a toddler in grown man's pajamas.

SHE HASN'T YET TOLD STEPHEN. She hasn't, in fact and of course, told anybody. The pain of miscarrying suddenly increases tenfold at the thought of not being able to speak about it. When she looks in the mirror she is clearly not pregnant anymore.

The hot, blossomed life-force is gone.

Violet knows it is her fault. If she had spoken about it to somebody, anybody, it would have been enough of a message to please come, sweetheart come. This filament of her imagination had nowhere to go. There was no "us," no "mommy and daddy" for the baby to attach to. She hasn't told Stephen because she knows it will mean the end of their affair. She hasn't told Bill because she doesn't know whether Stephen loves her because she is Violet Elizabeth Roe or because she is Bill's wife, conveniently living only a few doors down the street.

THE FOLLOWING MORNING, still cramping and having to change her sanitary pad every few hours, Violet drops her children off at Stephen and Flo's, and takes a cab to one of London's many airports.

By 2 o'clock she is flying over France. By the time she touches down in Rome she has read *The Italian Saga*—

twice—and learned to speak Italian fluently. She leaves her Englishness behind, if not in one of London's many airports, then in the plane itself, donning her eighteenth century garb and leaving the airport with a stream of acned young men embarking on the Grand Tour.

Violet has never left England before. She's gone to the end of Brighton Pier, which was longer than she expected, but that doesn't really count as leaving the country. She's never gone to Ireland or Scotland or Wales. She's gone inside and she's gone outside and she's gone monkeys' tails, but only in primary school and that was no further than just outside Rebecca's and Edith's elastic ankles. She's climbed up to the dome of Saint Paul's Cathedral, something she'd never want to do again, and that's as far up as she's ever gone. Never in an airplane and certainly never in a hot air balloon or a zeppelin, but who gets to do such wondrous things?

Bill has been abroad. In the war. Does that count? He spent most of his time cooped up inside a plane trying to hear above the sound of the engine the messages being sent to him from the ground. He was in the RAF and used to lie to girls, who could sniff out men in uniform from a mile off, that he piloted planes and released bombs on Germans having dinner in their houses, Germans on their bicycles, Germans making out for the first time behind sheds, on benches, in the cupped palms of sand dunes. Really, he just operated the radio and injected dying friends with morphine.

He spent most of the war flying back and forth across the English Channel without even knowing where he was. Was there turbulence on those flights? Did the pilots get a little silly and start wiggling their planes about in the sky like dancing bees? Violet had once been interested in asking Bill about the war and he'd once been interested in telling her stories, but those days ended when Madame was born.

VIOLET IS NOT A MOTHER ANYMORE. Or a wife. She is younger and prettier than she's ever been. Not a single hair on her head has been coloured or lost to age or alopecia. Her eyebrows are cleanly arched. Her teeth are sparkling white. Her miscarriage is yesterday's news.

Mia is nowhere to be seen, but no matter. Piranesi is around. As is his team of homeless extras. The streets are occupied. Every placard has something to say. Violet doesn't think twice about where she is going, finds herself ten years old again in some preteen castle fantasy with her arms around Keats's watery tomb. Keats and Shelley and first-name-basis Mary and all the dead babies and all the short-lived lives hover over the graveyard.

Here and now she can be anyone, but she forgets that it is too late to be a child prodigy or a young superstar of letters. She is inside *The Italian Saga,* so far away from Stephen and her grey loss, his ordinariness growing starchier by the second. Her hair, failing, falling, being let go of; her bedside table with its paperback copy of *Madame Bovary* that she has dusted every Saturday for god knows how many months; the bucket of pee- and poop-stained nappies soaking in the bathroom, all mean nothing to her here. Here is youth, sex on the rise, sparkling eyes and teeth, the space and time to saunter. The glare from all the hot dusty tin-can cars that stream along on their merry way to nowhere cannot compete with Violet's radiance.

She arrives just in time to take the cast of *The Italian Saga* into her loving arms and make her damp and drizzly London life disappear entirely. She is not Violet of the Kitchen or Violet of the Lavatory Bowl Cleaning Powder or Violet of the Put the Towels in the Airing Cupboard. She is whoever she wants to be, her cheeks slightly red from the sun, freckles springing up joyously. She is the one who can navigate this traffic of grand tourists, this Roman holiday. Her shoes are new but they do not give her blisters because characters aren't real.

Sixteen

PIRANESI TAKES VIOLET TO SKIRT SOME RUINS. He takes a photograph of her beside Cestius' pyramid. She is glowing today, her hair moving about her face in the breeze, her skin already sending forth the freckles of a trip to the south will do the trick. She has left her identity in London, along with her Emma Bovary boredom.

It is a warm September day. This is new love, full of respect and you first, no, you first, you coy little smiley face topped with kisses. She is falling in love with Rome because nobody expected her to. They expected her to die lonely in a flat in Hackney with her wig askew. Not at all. It is so much more to walk in between two cities, two lives. Real life. Fiction.

We are here and we are not here, she thinks.

IN EUROPE WE GET ONE LIFE ATOP ANOTHER. The kabob house beside the house with the small front door because people actually used to be that short. All of them. Except giants. The cathedral built on holy ground and blessed with holy water next door to the department store blessed with Mega Blow Out Sales! and automatic flushing toilets on every floor.

The people live among the ruins like it's nothing special. Cell phones buzz into the styrofoam hands of tourists that brush the master's piece. Sirens and car stereos blare through the ruined bodies of laughing harlots running from puffing, red-faced senators, everybody's sandals slap-slapping. The incredibly loud beeping of the garbage truck echoes in the ancient square. A hose pipe noses garbage along the invention of the aqueduct. They speak the names of the sacred places so haphazardly—"Meet you at The Angel in 45"—and tie their shoelaces in the dandelion-ridden remains of *History Book.*

VIOLET STANDS BESIDE THE PYRAMID and patiently waits for Piranesi to fish his camera out and turn it on.

"Smile! You're on holiday."

The Romans got used to living in the carcass of a fallen city, picked at by the elements, gawked at by its guests, so that the number of clean tablecloths the waiter has today or the price of a pack of cigarettes at a particular shop have more significance than the fact that this is ancient history that we're talking about, people. Hush! You're in a crypt, with important ghosts, with the breath of a gladiator on your neck, the swish of the expat's Halloween toga sliding over your parting thighs.

Violet is part of history in her smoking conversation with Piranesi. They sit together on the same steps that once felt the flip-flop of a general's sandals. His mistress fell on these same stone steps that Violet stubs her cigarette out on, chipped a tooth and blamed him for making her come to meet him.

Piranesi sits down beside Violet on the cool stone.

"Why have you come here, Vi?"

"Just needed a break. From the kids. From Bill."

"That's all?"

"Not really. I keep opening *Madame Bovary*, only to be interrupted by one of them waking up or the potatoes coming to a boil. I've only read one chapter."

"So?"

"I'm just bored."

"And that's your biggest worry? Come on, Violet. You should see how some of my figures spend their days. Their nights!"

"I've got my worries, they've got theirs. My house is small. My hair is leaving me, strand by beautiful strand. My husband is a dullard. What else is a wife supposed to feel?"

"Joy. Love. Tenderness. Closeness. All of these. All the time."

"Alright then," says Violet, smiling. She stands, takes Piranesi's hand and leads him into Flaubert's cool church.

Tale of the Small Green Weeds

III

OUR TOURIST FEET TRAVEL OVER STONES traveled over by people now dead. The resent causes blisters. Our togas erode the topography of the consumerist state. In all our oil-fed dreams we hurtle majestically in our streamlined fantasies of rayon, polyester and other life-affirming fabrics.

The plastic is as smooth as a speech. Our warriors erupt from wet bushes in their MEC equipment. This mountain is a mute relative loved by a scrawling array of anoraked believers.

Stone must be quarried and heaved over rocky ground by the extras from *The Prince of Egypt* while the senator and wife fork strands of Easter basket plastic—yellow, purple, pink—into their laughing mouths. Stone returns to sediment, surrenders to the probing tendrils of creepers, hangs out in the background of a foreclosure sign.

The cities are falling. One by one. Tourists and activists continue to make record on their [insert technology]. The widows of dead houses shoulder the dust of cremation in Greek agony. We will build another city in the wreckage, let photographers and art students dig their portfolios into the wounds of our unemployed houses.

Searching the Hypermarché for oversized plastic bottles

of fluorescence designed to nurse our tiny warrior babes, the frenzy of choice overwhelms us. Soup cans roll from the living room of Eliot's "Preludes," the birth of convenience curling out its wonder from the soles of her tired, yellow feet. How daintily, how systematically we bring the mountain to her knees with our plastic fingers.

This broken grid of love that crumbles in the wake of marketing executives coming through, ruling rightly, a people afraid to not complete the round trip including accommodation.

I rage here in my electric office at the mouthwatering rustle of man-made fibres fired at the nervous system of aquatic life, the tires burning in the pits of our insatiable bellies.

Bless the warriors as they scale the mountain in the rain, block the slick road from completing the circle from fracking field to check-out counter, Ma'am.

Seventeen

THE FIRST PICTURE Hilda is responsible for cataloguing comes from an institution in Rome. It is of a woman's body, headless, bent over a log, shaded much too lightly, with black pointy shoes that twist so far back both ankles appear snapped from their moorings. In the foreground and background are trees of the same size, shape, and colour. The figure dwarfs them, making Hilda think that the trees might in fact be root vegetable tops. There is a frog on the ground close to the place where the head would have been, almost as a replacement for the head. The picture is untitled but numbered. In the bottom right hand corner someone has written:

Name: Mia Italian Surname

Age: 17

Occupation: Catholic schoolgirl, *Hustler*, circa 1983

Hilda turns the picture over and holds it down hard with both palms as if she is trying to push it right into the table. *The Italian Saga* is so long and boring. Nobody in their right mind would spend anything but a beach holiday reading it. It contains over a hundred characters, most of them related, each hailing directly from a pasta sauce commercial. All the stereotypes that pop into your head when you hear the word *Italian* are hauled in as a good day's catch and sprinkled liberally over the pizza pages.

No matter how well Hilda prepares herself for the droning, monotonous voice of the narrator, no matter how many snacks, video games and unfinished patchwork quilts she brings, she will never be able to sit through *The Italian Saga* without first being knocked over the head with a wooden mallet. A light to medium tap only, just enough to give her a concussion, not enough to dent her skull.

Mia is everywhere. It can only mean one thing: that Hilda didn't read the book properly the first time around. Everyone else must have because they aren't being plagued by her. Jorgen probably read his with his eyes closed. Violet can't get enough of romance and violence so she would have finished hers in no time, while *Madame Bovary* waited patiently, too patiently, on her bedside table. Hilda doesn't even have to go through the whole list of characters to decide that they're all a bunch of goody-two-shoes that get their lines read on time. Hilda prefers to move on quickly from each experience, never hovering over the details, never jotting down the dates. Before this book, she went from one character to the next, never taking the time or energy to bond with anyone. In a heartbeat, she would just gather everyone up and give them anything they ever wanted, which would be everything plus one. Easy.

How Mia ended up in a mental hospital drawing bizarre pictures to pass the hours, Hilda has no idea. She doesn't even really care to know. Mia is perfectly well now. She's as clever as a fox, in fact, and is at this very moment sifting through the drawers of her cousin's marriage looking for clues to Hilda's hold over Jorgen, looking for cracks in their foundations to kick open with her yoga legs.

If Hilda wasn't so afraid to rock the boat, she'd smash Jorgen over the head with the vase on the mantelpiece—previously glued down to prevent this from ever happening—and go to London to stay with her future unborn granddaughter, Violet. After a few months of getting in Violet's way in the evenings and working in a department store during the day, she would have enough money to rent a small, damp flat close by. She would live out the rest of her days drawing pictures of her misconceived and miscarried children, smoking long brown cigarettes and wearing fingerless gloves. She would shop at the market and feed waterfowl and steal well-tended stuck-up blooms from public flower beds. Her name would remain Hilda, which children would attach to the word *hippo*. Deceivingly so because she would get skinnier with age until total strangers would wonder if her forté was bulimia or anorexia.

But this isn't to be Hilda's fate. She remains German and a little on the plump side. She attracts men way into her sixties. Her drawings progress to paintings progress to galleries and wealthy walls. One child does eventually come. Late, but better than never, smothered in baby-shower blue. Her marriage goes on and on and on, right to the grave in fact, and neither Mia nor a slew of other sows can undo the Boy Scout knots of fictional matrimony. There is no need at all to pity Hilda because she can pop in and out of sagas, romances, thrillers, and detective stories. She does short stints here and longer ones there. She butters her own bread and works magic into the winter of Jorgen's heart so that he jingles along beside her like a red setter in a dog food commercial.

HILDA BRINGS THE DOCTOR A CUP OF TEA. She places it on a saucer to indicate that she considers him not interesting in that way. Beside the tea she places Mia's picture.

Without looking up, the doctor says, "You know that girl needs help."

Hilda doesn't want to have this conversation.

"Are you planning on helping her?" asks the doctor, turning to face Hilda, studying her face in that really unnerving, invasive way that feels mildly sexual.

"Not really."

"Why not?"

"She'll figure it out eventually."

"Figure out what?"

"That Jorgen loves me, not her."

Eighteen

VIOLET FEELS LIKE A CAGED ANIMAL. Madame Bovary and Tom Sawyer are both going through *difficult stages*. Madame has started to bud breasts and Tom has started to pinch puppy fat. He waits for his sister behind every corner, jumping out so effectively that he never fails to scare the living crap out of her.

Tonight is Halloween and Violet is taking the evening off to meet a friend for a drink at the Monarch's Body Part. Tom has warned Madame that as soon as their mum leaves the house she will be subjected to a series of "really horrible events" that will "chill her blood" and leave her "begging for mercy." Madame has been pleading with her mother all afternoon not to go out, but Violet has made it clear that she will not have them ruin her evening yet again!

It is almost 8 o'clock and Violet is standing before the hallway mirror concealing her smoke-wrinkled lips under dark red lipstick and trying to ignore her daughter's guilt trip. Madame sips tea from a mug in between pleas, making her whole argument a lot less convincing.

"Please, mum. I'm scared. He's going to do something to me." *Slurp*. "Something horrible. Please tell Susan you can't go. Please!"

At this exact moment, Tom springs from the hall closet brandishing blood-stained Dracula teeth. Violet nicks a tooth with her lipstick and Madame screams her loudest, fakest scream, while letting her hand accidentally throw the tepid contents of her tea mug right at her mother's skirt and legs and nylons, shoes.

"Right. That's it you two! Bloody little shits! Get to your rooms. Now!"

Madame whacks her brother around the head. Hard. Then runs to her bedroom shouting "I hate you both!" Tom looks at his mum, goes to speak, but can't because his teeth are too big. Sucking loudly to rein in the dribble that is already escaping from his mouth, he goes off to his room and shuts the door.

Violet goes into the living room and sits down. She stands up again and pulls her nylons down, slips her ridiculous who'd-look-at-me-in-these heels? off and then rolls the nylons into a damp ball. She sits there, slouched, rolling the nylons around and around, like dough. Susan won't even notice I'm not there. That cow'll talk to anyone who'll listen. And I call her my friend. I don't even have any friends.

Violet lights a cigarette, leans back in her chair and closes her eyes. The first drag is heaven. It takes all the tension from her body and expels it on the exhale.

It's raining. She didn't realize how hard. The distance between her and a night out is growing larger. It's too late to change now and her only other nylons without holes are too thin and won't go with these shoes, and anyway Madame won't let me hear the end of it if I abandon her. Why can't they just get along?

She hears Susan knocking on the door. "You in there, love?" she coos through the letter box. There is a long pause followed by a second knock. Violet holds her breath and winces, sinking further into the armchair. Soon she hears the sound of heels clicking off into the night.

SHE'S IN THE SAME ROOM that Hilda and Bill were in earlier. She belongs here too. With the rain. In the orange hum. With the tacky bric-a-brac. The only difference is that she doesn't dare even think about what she could do to improve her life. It has been over a year since she's seen Stephen and almost five years since Bill left. The walls are yellowing from the smoke. The net curtains need bleaching. She'd do it if she cared, but she doesn't. She wouldn't care if Bill walked through the door right now and said, "Trick or treat?"

She wouldn't say anything. Not a single word. She'd just shout down the hallway at the children, "Your father's home!"

Nineteen

LONG AFTER HIS MARRIAGE TO VIOLET, according to the cassette tape whirring in the machine, Bill develops a strange, uncensored love for a woman who works the scarves and handbags counter at Selfridges.

They meet in the usual way: over a wife's birthday gift. The colours of the scarf worry Bill, but he takes the woman's word for it that they are both "chic" and "modern." At this point the woman gets given a name—Hilda—and a story of her own: husband lost to adultery; ticking maternal clock; red hair; large breasts.

In the end, Bill only needs the time between one tea and scone meeting on the fourth floor and the next to make his decision.

"Of course, love. Of course I'll do it."

They meet at her flat the following Thursday night. Hilda is crying when she opens the door. She has been crying on and off all afternoon. The dismal weather does nothing to lessen her sadness. This is not the way it is meant to happen. What if it doesn't take? How will she raise a child all by herself? What will her family say?

Bill is all "hush, hush," one hand reaching under her skirt, the other stroking her little shush girl hair. In theory, over two-lumps-please tea, the act seemed sweet to him, a duty that any good man would honour without hesitation. But here and now, standing by an almost bare coat rack, rain slashing the frosted glass of the front door, he sees that it is only about sex.

It takes just the one meeting to impregnate her. Bill waits for her to call him to have a second go, but she never does. He returns to her flat hoping to bump into her on her way home from work. After three tries he gives up. One Saturday afternoon he goes to her work and hovers around outside watching her stroke silk cornflowers over the cheek of a businessman. Months later he sees her in the street, her blue coat, her bump, her head scarf bought at half price, cigarette smoke leaking from her nostrils. Eventually, as the memory of his encounter with Hilda begins to lose its sharp edges, he reverts back to believing that his actions had been nothing but noble all along. Noble sweetness in the whispered corners of her hair.

FATHERLESS, the baby boy lives at the mercy of his mother's depressions and fits of rage that stem from having to stuff emotions for the scarf and handbag-buying public. He grows up to be a pathetic man, locked forever in a Piranesi etching, pitied by art students and gallery visitors alike.

A few years pass and Bill decides to send a cheque for 50 pounds to the department store. Not knowing her surname, he addresses it to "Hilda—the Scarves and Handbags Lady." It is returned to him a week later with a note: "Mrs. German

Surname no longer works for Selfridges. We regret to inform you that she left no forwarding address." Bill rips the note up into as many tiny pieces as his TV Drama producer will allow. Then kicking the leg of the sofa until he is crying heavy onto the carpet, he realizes that he has lost all his children without a fight.

Twenty

TOM SAWYER, LONGHAIRED, sandalwooden, in the dark of a makeshift bed, pulls his new woman closer. It's the early hours of the morning, 1970s London.

Days are longer than they used to be. The street doesn't burst open after the first drink like it once did. A child is pulling on the arm of the new woman. He's hungry. He wants his breakfast.

Tom stays in bed most of the day most days. He doesn't want to look for a job. The rejection is repetitive. Violet all over again, pushing him out of the way so she can charge upstairs to throw up, pushing him out of the way so she can pick up her fallen wig, roadkill on the living room rug, that he lovingly bends for to save her bald head from blushing.

BY TEN IN THE MORNING the landlord arrives to kick them out. He stands in the doorway between the rainy day and Tom's family scurrying around to collect their belongings. Boxes and suitcases and plastic bags and quilt covers stuffed with all that they have. Toothbrush beside teddy bear beside spider plant beside rolled up poster beside knickers beside joss sticks beside dogeared novel beside Japanese bowl beside LP beside boy, almost five, little body tight with stress and fear.

They go to Violet's place because there is nowhere else to go. She lives in a block of flats in Hackney, but despite her hundreds of neighbours, she knows nobody by name. Madame Bovary is still at home. She has grown out of her lustrous flesh and become quite ordinary. She brings in the rent money and a little extra. When she leaves for work in the morning, Violet is smoking by the yellow curtains. When she gets back, her mother is in the same spot looking out the tenth floor window at dead grass trodden muddy by pissed-off kids. The waste land stretches out into the fingers of future city planners, into poems that have already been written, but for now it is Madame Bovary's kingdom of coming and going. Violet focuses on her daughter's fat. "Thighs like Bill's," she thinks.

Bird in the cage. Sticks in the joints. Food left hanging on its last legs. The warm milk fattening the cup of her imagination, filming her old beak. Her skin the bark of trees that line the murderer's ravine. Her dreams trapped in the twisted dance of a Tesco bag out on the commons. The pissed-off kids' football clanging against the wall, their rough howls savaging her migraine deep into the night.

"Why's the light off?" Tom asks, bringing in the light of his small family and their lives in bags and boxes.

The new woman's boy goes over to the window and looks out. He sees that there are kids outside, playing. They will have wide-rimmed teeth mouths. They will smell of sweat and soap and their mothers' perfume and grass stains mingled with the smell of rain coming and the pink drool of gobstoppers. They will look him up and down. Dare him to come closer.

"You can set up in Madame's room. She's going to stay with

Susan for the weekend. You won't need more than that, will you?" Violet asks, looking directly at the new woman and then at the boy.

"Should be plenty. I'm going out. Need anything, anyone?" Tom makes it to the fifth floor stairwell before having to crouch down in a corner to breathe into his hands, into his T-shirt pulled up over his mouth. His chest is ripped with lines of anger, spreading hot tendrils up under his left armpit. Digging his fingers into the pain he springs up, suddenly, to let a woman and her two children pass. The woman has seen men in these stairwells plenty of times—doubled over, sleeping, even dead. She pushes her children ahead of her, shoving them up and out of the way, snapping at them to "get a move on!"

VIOLET SAYS THEY CAN MAKE TEA, but the new woman says, "It's OK. I'm just going to set up in Madame's room." The boy follows her in and they shut the door and talk in whispered voices about where to put things and where not to put things. From time to time the boy opens the bedroom door and slips off down the hallway to collect another box or bag or sack. This one is too heavy for him. He calls to his mum and she hurries out of the bedroom shushing him and grabbing at the bag. After they are finished, she lies down on the bed and asks him to lie down beside her. She curls his little body up into the C of her own and strokes his hair. Within minutes the two of them are sleeping off Tom's smoke-shrouded weird mother and the brutality of London's children.

VIOLET HAS THE TYPE OF MIND THAT SCURRIES. Each option gets nibbled first then spat out, little dark brown droppings left here and there. Underwater, everything gets washed clean. And begin again.

Poverty doesn't help. And we're not talking about the kind of poverty that turns your body into a walking corpse *à la* Piranesi. We're talking about living just below the poverty line and not even noticing it until just after Christmas, or when someone in the family is really sick and can't work, or when somebody has or does something extra special that you will never, ever have or do. The rest of the time you do your routine routinely while the real poor wait in the alley for you to have a party's worth of empty cans and bottles.

But all the time, as you live nudged just below the measuring stick, there is an underlying buzz of anxiety that shapes every thought, crooked or stiff. Proper breathing goes out the window. "Whatever will be, will be" is replaced by "What if?" Digestion never functions optimally.

THE BLANKETS COME UP TO VIOLET'S CHIN. She stays in bed, nursing her throbbing entitlement. She pulls the blankets around her skinny body, tighter, tighter, so tight she steals the covers from her own feet, pulls the blankets so tight around her crackling head that she can hardly breathe. There, in the hot dark, she tries to turn her thoughts into breath. She manages three exhales, three inhales before she is racing off into life is hard, life is terribly hard.

Tale of the Small Green Weeds

IV

THE REFUGEE SHEPHERDS HIS FAMILY against an available wall. They build their home in a covered walkway beside a surge of holidaymakers that promise all hell will be paid to the travel agent for sending them to this filthy refugee camp. This isn't a holiday! With these cockroaches stumbling up the beach and making me spill coconut oil on my paperback! Trust us to pick the Greek island closest to their capsized bloody boat!

This is the fear of death under a magnifying glass.

He tries to shield his daughters from the fat peering eyes of tourists wheezing past in their sweaty encasements, off to spend money on jugs of beer and calamari. He eats. His family eats. There is no roar of war. The night is quiet, except for the shouts of holidaymakers, too drunk to notice the calendar-ready scenes of whitewashed walls and geraniums. The hibiscus bush shimmies in the night air, a donkey haws against the shushing of waves. The man's daughters manage to sleep, although they stir frequently, their legs kicking at the blankets, their tiny groans of sorrow lost on a whole world of sleepers.

They keep their living quarters clean. Sweep constantly.

Try to be as inconspicuous as possible. He scouts out bread and cheese with the other fathers and they pay for it out of their Ziploc'd life savings. By the end of the week the men have found a farmer looking for labourers he can exploit before the state gets hold of them and gives them rights.

Here he gets stuck. Listening to the familiar sounds of the sea. The beep of angry horns at rush hour. The rustle of shopping bags. He lives here at this place without an address. Always outside. Waiting for bottles of water, waiting for work, for morning, away from nightmares and into the warmth of car exhaust, shoes passing on the pavement moving the bodies of these tourists that are outraged by line-ups and delayed flights, by window seats and aisle seats and irons that don't work and towels that look ratty, by extra baggage fees and unclean rooms and crowded pools and missing ice cubes and straws that have tiny slits in them so that they don't suck properly, by beggars coming into the lobby, by taxi drivers who take the long route, by tea that isn't hot and margarine that comes instead of butter, by the great inconvenience of pneumatic drills and cockerels and donkeys and foghorns and refugees speaking in tongues with their ten children's one hundred gypsy fingers sliding the gold right off my bloody finger!

He watches his daughters, each of them, both of them, stay close to their mother on their cardboard house, playing with each other's hair, wrapping shawls around each other's shoulders. He thinks about his father's dusty body. Still. Easily rolled over. Made lighter by age, by the rationing that has gone on for years, with the war. He sees his mother, her body following his father's in crumpled broken exhaustion, all elbows, fingers wringing, toes, snot in the dust, a marriage annulled by an explosion. He imagines his parents here, seeing his family stuck against this wall, waiting, being eyed up and down or looked at with pity and handed strange food in carrier bags. He thinks of the family he left behind. Crammed into refugee camps. Fighting. Staring at walls. Staring at the sides of tents. Staring at the ground.

Twenty-One

HILDA IS OVER THE HILL according to the women in her local grocery store who regard her bump with wide eyes. She is already in her third trimester and cannot understand why nobody has noticed until now. When she looks at her body in the mirror it is like looking at another woman's body. Everything is wider, plumper, redder. Even her eyes look different.

Mia has gone back to her ocean of a saga. Hilda hardly thinks about her now. She thinks about other women. New, fresh specimens that she finds talking to Jorgen at his workshop when he doesn't know she's watching, after the work is done, while their husbands are inspecting Jorgen's handiwork. Today Hilda, feeling like a lovesick school girl, hangs back in the air of the street, wishing her footsteps had been loud enough to alert her husband to her arrival, wishing she hadn't come at all. Gone are the days of cell phones, she laments. I could have told him I was coming and he would have turned that Mrs. away with her red polka dot skirt spinning a design on him, and her hair, fingers of snakes on the breeze.

It took her too long to get pregnant. By the time it happened, over fifteen years after they started trying, she was in her forties and on her way out of the world. Years of breathing in Violet's cigarette smoke had done a number on her skin. Being pregnant made her young again.

Today she is sensitive. After being stared up and down the aisles of the grocery store, she does not want to be standing here looking at Jorgen flirting with somebody's wife. Without considering how silly she will look if he looks up and sees her, she turns and hurries away. Once out of eyeshot, she slows her pace until she finds herself standing stock still on the pavement not knowing where she is going or where she should go. At home she will have to face the darkening afternoon rooms that swell with the sound of ticking clocks that she keeps forgetting to hack to pieces with an axe.

She begins to walk again, as suddenly as she had stopped, heading out of the village towards the downs, riding a pony, riding a donkey, feeling twelve and bright with princess blood, her baby tucked snug inside her. The path is wet with rain, with parts so muddy that she must hop around them, hanging on to fence posts or tree trunks for balance. After a while, she stops caring about her shoes and just lets the mud ooze and splatter them until even the hem of her skirt is peppered with brown dots.

By 6 o'clock, in winter moonlight, she reaches the next village. She enters the only pub in the village, orders all things greasy, and then chases the meal into her stomach with a silky line of dark ale. Her baby throbs for more so she orders a second pint and is woozy after only one sip. She pushes the drink to the other side of the table and stares at the light it doesn't have within it. Her food-smeared plate repulses her, so she turns it over, prompting the landlord of the pub to hurry over and remove it. The beer she is drinking doesn't concern him, nor the cigarette she is at this moment filching from

Violet's open handbag. It is the absence of a man that leads him to whisper his concern along the oak slab of the bar, upsetting the ash in the ashtrays and making his regulars cough.

NEEDING AIR AND NARRATIVE, Hilda steps out into the quiet village. She realizes she is conveniently close to the doctor's house and decides to visit him. Once out of the village, she turns and looks back on the landscape. Village, hill sloping down, moonlight everywhere it can possibly get its sticky paws, its gaping maw. She can see a train snaking through the valley below, luminous with businessmen with nice breath on their way home from the City. For a moment she lets her mind wander over their trousered arses, their fine stubbled necks, the sheer magnitude of their tallness. She burns her eyes into their laughing faces, grips on in her sudden raw delight at their fucking bodies in and out of suits and conversations and revolving glass doors.

Is this the train or other fast moving vehicle that I'm supposed to throw myself in front of? she thinks. This one? Full of gorgeous, young stockbrokers?

THE TRAIN IS MOVING IN SLOW MOTION. Mouths are opening and then they are closing, hands are moving in the air to the beat of conversation, wallets are opening, money is fanning the hot faces of these commuting geniuses. The saliva on their teeth is hanging in beaded lines that quiver in the laughing breath of vice, the flab of the passive voice.

Hilda starts to run—to the best of her third trimester ability—in the dark on a downhill slope with slight heels through an obstacle course of molehills and cow pats.

This is it, she thinks. This is the heroine dead on the tracks scene. This is the mother-to-be racing towards the last page. This is the end of me.

She is nearing the track. The train, such a slow, slow train, even slower now to compensate for a pregnant character, is edging closer. She can see the pin stripes on the men's suits, their eyes turning to watch her, their fingers starting to point. One has his window open and is shouting at her in a deep drawl. Even the driver has seen her, has pulled the whistle and is gearing down to stop the train. There will be one hell of a soft plop when she falls under this iron serpent.

Hilda steps onto the track and holds out her arm, index finger stretched out to lightly touch against the stopping, now stopped train. Her baby beats his fists inside her.

The men pour out onto the embankment in fast motion, their black legs bellows of confusion.

In real time Hilda steps out from in front of the train to face the men gathering on the bank, smoking, resuming their conversations, attempting to fold their gigantic newspapers.

"I needed to stop you," says Hilda to the train driver, our working class hero. "They are moving too fast. I didn't want to see any more destruction, for this one's sake." She circles her belly with her palm.

"You can't stop this lot," says the driver, lighting a cigarette and offering it to Hilda.

"I can see that. But it may have been worth a try."

"Were you going to top yourself, Miss?"

"I was supposed to. That was my duty, my great act of service to my sex, you know. But, as you say, it wouldn't have done much to hold back these Hounds of Progress."

The train driver knows exactly what Hilda is talking about. He's been ferrying these dirty scoundrels and their egos back and forth for years.

"Look around you," Hilda says to the driver, handing back the cigarette. "Look at these sexy trousered ones. They're everywhere and they can't stop talking about themselves. We haven't come very far at all. I'm still here to die under a train. Nobody will remove that bit, even if I bring in a lawyer."

"Well, we could just pretend it happened."

"We could? How?"

"You just lie there and we can start this again."

Hilda lays down on the tracks, arms splayed in their own random ways, legs scissoring out into Crime TV territory.

The train driver takes off his hat and bows his head. The stockbrokers notice what he is doing and crowd over to the front of the train where they see Hilda, dead to the world, her poor baby dead, too.

"Help me move her, lads," shouts the driver, and together with three tall men drenched in cologne, they tip her off the tracks and down the bank. There is a splash as she lands in a shallow stream.

"That will do for next week's episode," says the driver, flicking his cigarette into the worst forest fire in German history, and climbing back onto the train.

FROM AN AERIAL VIEW, we note that the men are like baby spiders scurrying back up onto the train. They are already talking about tomorrow's stock prices rising and falling like Hilda's chest as she plays dead and thinks about a hot bath and squeaky clean lemon shampoo hair.

Twenty-Two

IT IS TOO LATE TO PAY SOMEONE A VISIT by the time Hilda reaches Dr. Grebing's house, but she waits only a few seconds before she is ushered in, muddy as a dog, and taken to the fireside to warm up.

"I'm a whale!"

The doctor laughs.

She throws a cushion at him.

"Where's your wife?"

"Dead and buried."

"Oh, up the churchyard, is she?"

"Yep," mumbles the doctor, around the stem of his pipe, being lit, at this moment, as we speak, giving off the smell of masculine and far, far away.

Dr. Grebing's wife is still very much alive, living in the capital with one of her husband's more irritating interns, all cocktails and scarves and Japanese screens and wide-angled rooms, set-decked modern and minimalist. Everywhere petals just dropped.

"Where's your husband?" asks the doctor.

"Flirting." She throws another cushion at him. She wants to hit him in the face, wants to knock his glasses off, graze his skin with the zipper.

"Stop it!" he yells, sounding pubescent and raw.

Hilda looks at the doctor straight on with her most serious face. "What's the matter?"

"I hate that you're having his child."

"His child? You mean my husband's child? Whose child should I be having?"

"Mine."

"You already have five of your own."

"All brats!"

They both laugh at this and the room comes over all jolly with Christmastime and the doctor even takes it upon himself to turn the television on to the Yule Log channel so that they now have both a real fire and a fake one blazing in the same room.

"Which do you prefer?" he asks Hilda.

"They both have their merits," she says. "The real one has somebody's sweat behind it. Maybe somebody handsome, bare-chested even. The fake one has intelligence. It can bring instant holiday spirit to an otherwise neutral room."

The doctor is thinking.

"Yes," he says, "and it is nice to have two fires going in a single room. I'd never even tried it before now but it did cross my mind earlier on today that it might be worth trying, and then when I saw you there soaked through and miserable, I just had to give it a go."

Hilda likes the doctor these days, but she wonders if all this alone time has the potential to twist him into his old self. The failed artist turned art collector who spent years completely oblivious to the needs of his loved ones and staff. He was a tired old bull, with torn pieces of vegetable matter hanging from his horns and no hands to remove it.

The change came when he left the hospital. His wife left him a few days later, unable to continue her affair in secret with him home every day of the week, and his children, who had been long out in the world, all got waylaid by some writer or other and sucked up into more exciting novels. He felt truly alone.

But the man he became pleased Hilda. He was brighter around the eyes and spent days at a time exploring the nearby countryside, sleeping out under the stars with a grass stalk between his teeth, hanging fish and game on hooks and painting them still. Life. Pomegranate. Bee. Blue and white broken china. The shrunken head of a forgotten lemon.

He wants to woo her, even though she is clearly only here to have her portrait painted, as he promised her weeks ago; only here to have him touch her on the shoulder in a fiery way, one touch, brief, uncomplicated. She is a free woman. Free from the shackles of institutional ground rules, free from the husband's hands and arms, his tightening grip, free from Biology and God. She can go anywhere with anyone. Her feet carry her. Her legs move so well. She is always coming over a hill. She is always a dot in the distance coming in from a storm. She is everything he needs her to be.

"Let's start, Doctor."

The doctor looks at her with such sadness in his eyes that she feels her insides tighten. All her tenderness flakes miserably away or is too busy in the womb to have energy for anyone else, especially aging doctors in their shabby dressing gowns.

"Yes, of course. I'll get my paints and things."

Paints and things. He always says "paints and things."

Twenty-Three

HILDA HAS BEEN IN A BAD MOOD ALL DAY. She has said "no" to everything when she could have just as easily said "yes." Wisely, she has tried to remove herself from the situation, to perch on the edge of the Time Out Chair teetering softly between falling and sitting comfortably. Back and forth, gently rocking like a toy in a nursery after the smash and roar of children has gone. She only rocks like this when she is crying. She only cries like this when she thinks about her will to conceive and her body's lack of creativity. The test she took last winter at the institute concluded that she was never creative to begin with. Once out of eye-shot of the graduate student who was conducting the test, she tore the paper up and threw it into a bush. The smug face of the student stayed with her for weeks afterwards. "So, you want to be an artist? Well, according to our study, and it is 95 percent accurate, you lack in the creativity department. You're great at organizing and planning, though. And you're very good with people. Have you thought about becoming a nurse?"

"I am a nurse."

"Oh, yes, of course. It's written right here." The student runs her finger along the word *nurse*, then passes the paper across the table to Hilda.

"There. You can show the results to your husband."

"What husband?"

"Oh, I'm sorry. I thought it said that you were married."

"Right. Yeah. I am."

The two women look at each other for longer than they are supposed to.

"Are you OK, Mrs. German Surname?"

"Are you?"

"I asked first."

"I asked second . . . No. I'm not OK. My test results tell me that I am destined to wipe people's asses. They tell me that I should give up while I'm ahead."

"Why are you ahead?"

"Because I still have my looks."

"Yes. You are more beautiful than you are kind. Or clever."

"I know. That is what people have always told me."

They pause to look deeply into one another's eyes. The graduate student looks away first.

"Why are you so sad?" Hilda asks.

"I just am. Everyone in my family, going way back, is sad."

"I'm sad too. Right here and now and when I return home or when I start my shift tonight, I will be sad. As sad as you are right now, if not sadder. There is a gaping hole that has replaced most of me." Hilda stands and lifts her blouse to show the student what she means. The student can see through the large hole in her torso to the desk on the other side of the room. Strangely, all she can think is that the desk looks cluttered and the rubber plant looks a little on the dry side.

"Where are your guts? Where's your intuition?"

"I don't know. There's just nothing there. It hurts so much, you know? There is nothing to live for. My marriage is flawed. I trip up on it daily. I slip around in it frantically, frightened that if I fall I'll never get up. My husband and I cannot agree on a single thing. This morning it was whether or not there was a raven or a crow on the garden fence. I don't even care who was right. I don't care that I don't like him and he doesn't like me. It's the other stuff that matters more. And now you tell me that I am not creative, which means I won't ever be an artist, which . . ."

"No! I did not say that."

"You did. You just told me that I was better off planning or caretaking or something."

"No. No. You have me confused with someone else. You are the most creative being I have ever met. Look at you! Look at your hair, flaming red like fire in a forest, spitting wildlife viciously. Look at your chin! It's the most creative chin I've ever seen. You are a walking canvas, Hilda. Sorry. May I call you Hilda?"

"Yes."

"Look. Here are your test results. You just need to turn them around and look at them upside-down. Everything fixes itself without you having to do anything at all."

The student slowly turns the paper around and pushes it towards Hilda.

"There."

HILDA STILL TEARS UP THE PAPER once she has left the building. She doesn't want the responsibility of being a creator. It's too much of a commitment.

For the first time, though, she can imagine a baby growing inside her. On her way home she stops at the toy store and buys a plastic doll, the most anatomically correct one she can find. She ties a thread around its torso and hangs it from a nail at the top of her gaping hole. As she walks, the hanging infant taps rhythmically against the inside of her blouse. *Boomph. Boomph.* All the way home.

Tale of the Small Green Weeds

V

THE WAR BROKE OUT ALL OVER HIS DREAMS. His wife and daughters pressed closer to the warmth of his inner wolf. But he could do nothing. He could not help anyone.

He wishes for window glass painted black to omit the day. Just the way the rain throws mottled insect hordes over the sheets. The sun is a great joke upon him.

When his women realize that the men in tall boots and protective gear aren't coming, all their fears are founded, built, and given flags. "Where are the burly men?" they ask.

THE HOUSE OF HIS DREAMS IS ALWAYS FRESHLY PAINTED, kitchen from a show room, rose-heavy arbour to shield the wedding guests from the guts of clouds, garden landscaped, weedless, lush. Everyone comes over to lick the taste of candy out of the walls and roof tiles. A gravel driveway graces butlers and maids in formation. A gong! The screen door thwacks behind a white woman in a cardigan, pulled tight against the gentle but chilly breeze. The breeze! Shield her from the breeze!

Twenty-Four

VIOLET IS ALL THE FINE LINES and sharp angles that I have inherited, the tendency to lose weight during illness and retain water when pregnant, the craving for tobacco and vinegar. Look at her face, so befitting of London in the 1940s, half hidden by bad processing, half obscured by the shaky finger of the photographer; half in the light, half stolen from the light by the shadow of her own house.

Violet is two women. The one before the cancer and the one after.

I began in her arms, pressed against her chest, listening intently for a ray of hope in among her lung lumps; listening to black, and the blues twanging against her rib cage.

I threw myself at her dying body in my recently come-alive one. Not just alive as in with a pulse getting from A to B, from one day to the next with my best foot forward, but as in fresh off the mother-boat with absolutely nothing to lose; alive as in "holy fucking shit that thing is alive!" A mouse on the run. A creature in the garden shed staring down the beam of a flashlight. I was on fire. A shooting flame of potential, flinging my body into the bed-ridden arms of my future heroine.

SUSAN ARRIVES. FRAZZLED.

"Oh Violet, sorry I'm late. Jack insisted that I make him a sandwich when he got off shift. Lazy bugger."

"You're not late. It's not even three yet."

"Bloody 'ell, you're right," she sighs, looking at the clock on the mantelpiece and sinking down into the too-low sofa at the same time. "What are those two up to? Bloody 'ell, Vi, this sofa is suckin' me under!"

Susan is a little on the heavy side. And she sweats. More than is normal. Her forehead is perspiring at the thought of the effort it will take her to get off the couch when the kids want something. She hauls herself up in preparation, preferring to be on her feet for when the time comes. She can take care of her own, but when it comes to other people's kids she gets anxious. She only does this because Violet takes her two in exchange.

"They're playing nicely in the back room. For once."

"So where you off to today?

"Just to the library."

"Nice. You picked a good day for it. It's bloody chuckin' it down out there."

"I know." Violet doesn't know if Susan is being sarcastic—why would anyone go outside in this weather?—or genuine—good day to be inside with a book.

There is a moment's pause as Susan registers that Violet is dressed in good shoes and a smart-looking dress. Her hair is hidden under a silk scarf; her lips beneath a brush of pale red lipstick.

"You look nice."

"Thank you," says Violet, walking to the door quickly. "I'll be back by five. If they're hungry, just give them some bread and butter. It's out on the sideboard. Bill won't be home until after me."

"Good. He might expect me to make him a sandwich!"

They laugh.

"Probably. So, I'll see you later then."

"Yep. Bye-bye love."

Violet takes her purse from the hall table, grabs an umbrella, and steps out into the street. We are in the realm of rain again. Rain and prying eyes. Susan has her face pressed up against the front room nets.

"Saucy cow," she thinks.

AS SOON AS VIOLET GETS AROUND THE CORNER she parks herself on the wet curb and puts her hazards on. Rain rivulets down her nylons. Now that she is wet she places her open umbrella on the pavement. She wipes her face when she sees Stephen coming, but it immediately starts streaming again with rain and makeup. He grabs her by the wrist like she is a child hanging from the grip of an angry parent and hauls her up off the curb. Then he wrings her out and puts her down on a dry page in Italy at the foot of a hill. So many varieties of butterfly and wildflower that London disintegrates on her tongue.

"Pfft." She plucks a fleck of grey matter from her lip. London tastes so unwell, she thinks. It cannot breathe. Like me, she thinks.

Stephen is beside a tree. He's a man. He's got man legs and man arms and a man chest. He's hard to the touch. Not in that way. Just hard to the touch all over, like his bones are closer to the surface than hers are. He's a kind of Jeremy Irons/George Orwell type. One that fucks like a goat in heat. His whole body is leaning towards death and sex simultaneously.

She squints her eyes to soften him, to fluff up his edges.

Now he can swing. Can breathe his rising chest up at the cheek of a child. Can exist outside of his sex. Can be a moment. A cherry could fall directly into his open mouth. A cherry could fall—*plip*—on the brim of his hat. Why does he stand like a lord of the field with his loins afire? Why does he pose for the photographer like a nude in clothing?

She knows it will be time to get back soon, but what is happening is good. The wind is in the pines, meddling. Their fire turns green and fey.

She takes everything she can get and then she asks for more. There are so many surfaces to be free against.

VIOLET AND STEPHEN ARE WALKING holding hands, turning their fingers around their fingers in circles. Poking out flesh messages into each other's palms. It's a glade. It's the shadow of a tree. It's the shade of all hell broke loose and scattered flowers over the hills. It's insects thrumming in the dry grass.

"Why are you wearing a string of pearls?" asks Violet

"A what?" Stephen touches his neck, feels the pearls there—How can they still be there?—and laughs loudly. He stops and turns to face Violet.

That morning his three-year-old had fastened Florence's pearl necklace around his neck. He barely felt her tiny fingers snap the clasp in place. He felt the necklace there afterwards. He even fingered it once. But in his rush to leave the house to meet Violet he forgot to remove it.

What a story! Who would believe that?

The pearls belong to Hilda. Filched from her dressing room. She enters, shivers out of the bracken and up Stephen's legs like a cold fever. Her red hair lights the dry grass and the fire spreads through the kingdom its hot fingers prying open the land. All harvest gold. All fields of waving gluten. All red leaves on water in their Japanese logic, bringing tidings of comfort and joy to the warren we call our global village. Heavy with plastic cracked into splinters and knives carving up all the lies that dare to cross its path, the village strains under the stench and mass of its sewage. The village rises up into tower after tower of concrete boredom-crime. Bury me, bury me, and then ferry the river water over me. I will rise again, covered in the glut and stew of the river bottom, slapping seaweed against the hull of a ship. *Plip. Plip.* Like a bird tapping at a window.

Hilda curls her hand around Violet's. They walk pretending not to know that they have crossed a line on a map drawn hundreds of years ago by the steady hand of a cartographer.

WHO'S GOING TO BE THERE TO WIPE ALL OUR BROWS when the fever is high? Who's going to bring the cool water of the song right to the mouth of our ears? What lover? What friend? What mother? All my characters suddenly find themselves kneeling at the bedside of the dying Violet. The nurse on duty would call this a breach of contract, a health hazard, a violation of code, but she's locked in the broom closet—what broom closet? Whoever heard of a broom closet in 2016?!—with her hands bound to a chair and her ankles bound to the same chair and a ball in her mouth and a strip of white tape (found on a shelf in the broom closet) over her HBO special mouth.

And that's it. We don't need her. Is she Hilda? We hope not. We don't need her in this time of Quaker silence and introversion. The group of characters sings in the tall grass around the hospital bed. A lion passes on his way to the other side of the savannah. Too many prayers hover over the bed. They clash and then they pour their hot tears over Violet's body until she is soaked through to the bone standing at the door to her house many years earlier. Not wanting to enter.

Susan sees her through the frosted glass and opens the door.

"Get in here! You're soaked right through."

Twenty-Five

HILDA WOULD NEVER WEAR A STRING OF PEARLS. They make her think of pencil-skirted women who are nothing without their Audrey Hepburn movies. That face. That darned face. She could squeeze it up into a ball and pop it into her mouth like a chocolate commercial. She can't take the funny girl thing seriously. It warps her fear of death, makes her think that a fashion spread equals immortality.

The pearls are put back into the prop box because they don't fit here. Silver fits. Some gold pieces would pass. Various precious gems would work. Amber being one because it's so thrilling to see an insect from another era, dressed in period costume, buzzing in some obscure tongue. But pearls are not OK. They are Republican tears suspended in thin air, on thin string, resting against the white gizzard of a Thank you, Ma'am. They cannot trespass over my live body into this novel.

REGARDLESS, AS IN WITHOUT REGARD, Violet persists that Hilda wear them anyway. In this scene.

Hilda finds them twirled thrice, because thrice is a word that is silly and must be said, around the neck of one of Madame Bovary's dolls.

The silent doll. The hard skin. The plastic reproduction of every woman's dream-nightmare spread across the wall like something heavy from Yeats's head. It came in the night, a small skin demon, bearing the weight of all my atrocities. They pick holes in her scalp and burrow in. They leave their eggs in hard to clean places. They teach her to check her heart for holes. Monthly. In front of the mirror. The bladder is coming out, falling down her leg, a heavy bag of slosh. The vagina kegels over and over, amen. But all along Hilda knows that the vein lines are turning into spiders and eating her poor supply of eggs. Speckled. Humbled. Raw. All the young mothers throw their fey legs into the air and birth warrior-style. She knows they will have to haul her in along with her shipwrecked soul, tits busting at the seams to get suckled, graying husband burying his mouth and nose in her sweaty hair.

HILDA, WITH HER PEARLS SWINGING LOW, waits impatiently in the bank line-up. She notes pens attached to their don't-steal-me tails, a floor mottled with the inner secrets of marble.

She is still waiting for her baby to be written into the plot. He hangs in the heavens like bible-thin paper, fluttery, covered with contradiction and poetry. She occasionally hooks him and he sometimes stumbles and is dragged along, bopping against cloud after cloud. But she hooks him wrong, through thin fabric, right at the fraying hem of his Huckleberry shorts. This doesn't stop her from casting Jorgen's hardening cock into her, waiting for him to stop grunting so that she can shove three pillows under her hips and wait there in the darkness of the bedroom. She pushes the sperm, one by millionth one, onward, his little soldiers, her little soldiers, forever loyal, forever ready to serve. She kneads and kegels and spasms them at her eggs. A stern dog trainer jerking at the puppy's leash in the name of good behaviour, forever. The dog will stop when you stop, wait beside you like a well-kept mistress while fluorescent tape flutters over her puppy brain, motorcycles whiz by spitefully, and horses clatter over Vienna's cobbles like girls hell-bent on ballet. Good girl!

Hilda's inner dog humps the leg of the man standing in front of her in the line-up. They step into some kind of dance. She doesn't care that she is panting, that her fingers have slipped under his silk-lined suit jacket and are reaching into the front of his pants. She doesn't care that he, without turning around—he doesn't want to miss the next free teller—has his fingers up her skirt, searching. By the time they get to the front of the line their dogs are fucking wildly, yelping gaily up at the chandelier, howling down the sign that reads *5% interest*. Relief. Free. Shards of window light piercing the lines of numbers that set you where you are meant to be. Ironed out and clad up in the corduroy sadness of T.S. Eliot with his biro.

"Sir?"

And he is gone as quickly as he snuck up against her mad and angry fingers.

"Next."

And she is gone too.

BANKS ARE DULL AND LIFELESS HAIR on a shampoo bottle label. Lather up the heads of the tellers. Tell them we are here and we can breathe life into marble and brass plate. We can shiver leather back into live animals galloping through a high-ceilinged London bank. Eliot at the window breathing on the frosted glass, waiting to rush out into the rain of his wife.

Twenty-Six

DR. GREBING KNOWS THAT HIS FIGURES will be championed by artists that have managed to stay off the street out of luck and the fact they possess mental illnesses that are easily masked by the insanity of capitalism. *Horror vacui* makes sure there is enough product to go around.

Hilda has been his assistant for over a year now. He has watched her with an irrational urgency that he takes home with him and spills around his marriage bed like ink in water. Her uniform is pressed to her skin. Her skin is pressed to her flesh. Her flesh envelopes her bones in complicated anatomy drawings. He colours her in, draws her to look at later. Fits her to his agenda, a pin of hope, a thought to have in the dark.

She dreams of him. Wakes up crying. They meet under a waterfall of willow leaves frosted by dew, evidence everywhere. She finds him crying into her hair in dreamscapes that defy logic. Up against gravity they move, like children on a trampoline, finding air and then losing it again.

THEY CHOOSE A HOTEL HALLWAY, where the carpet has no imagination, and the walls are of the most boring, boring you can imagine. They still breathe, but like babies that you hang your face over to check that they're not dead. They breathe like that.

Dr. Grebing can hear her. He's been listening for years. The raw threat of love has pushed him here, against the loyalty of his astrological sign. He must have the pleasure of her wish welling up, bloody and fresh, her pre-menopausal fire, against his darkling plain hooded soul.

He meets her, just as he promised he would. He doesn't even know if she will be there, as she promised she would. When he sees her he doesn't know what to feel. What if it isn't good? All this waiting can't pay off. What if she's neurotic? Hysterical? Vengeful?

He holds her for such a long time that she starts to cry.

"You came," she says, looking up at him.

THEY ARE SHY. Both feel the weight of their age, the ebb of their poise, the ridiculousness of new love. They remember their child-selves, fascinated and repulsed by the thought of their grandparents having sex. If they were watching this scene, they'd be judging. Surely. Surely this is not going to happen, with the pubis heading back to pre-pubescence, with the missing lubrication, with the world sagging its heavy judgment like a push of life through their senses.

But after an hour sitting side-by-side on the bed, they finally kiss.

It's not awkward. It's not embarrassing. It's tender, filmic, gentle. It's the kiss of a hundred years. The kiss of urgent love. Yes, love. In this pre-booked space of betrayal, love roams and then snaps its yawning shell jaws over them and makes everything dark and glorious.

For hours they play in the hotel bed. It is night by the time he opens the curtains and steps out onto the balcony to have the blessed smoke his wife won't ever allow him to have. She stays in the bed remembering all the years she waited with Jorgen's cum inside her for the sperm to wiggle frantically under the microscope of her good wife. Intending their way home. She lies there waiting for her whole life to break apart.

Twenty-Seven

HILDA IS LOOKING INTO HER MIRROR EYES. One hundred affirmations later and she looks the same. But spring is here and spring is the youth of the undergraduate English essay. It commands the clouds. This cloud is stone grey. This one is made by an angry pencil. This cloud flirts with the edges of the deep blue sea of sky. This is a cloud after rain, casting for sonnets in the lay of the verdant countryside.

SHE BURNS WHEN SHE THINKS of her husband's thighs. Rock steeples, bull horny, hairy as all Jesus. She swoons radically at the thought of her king, while the doctor is blown into some faraway landscape painting, a figure confined to the economic bracket of a field.

Jorgen must rise up from the grassy knoll, some kind of hawk that has been tamed by a young cold-air, autistic-bright mountain girl. He must rise to the occasion of Hilda's sex, Hilda's nursing breast. He must love her smell, even after babies have come out of that thing. He must nuzzle there in his bear-man outfit, which is really a bear-woman outfit because bears are feminine and rule the women's palpitating sweat lodge hearts.

Jorgen is fire walking along the road in its finest suit. Jorgen is water determined to erode doubt. His feet tread the earth. Air.

"I cannot stand the wait anymore," says Hilda, sniffing the mirror for her scent. "He needs to put that bear-woman suit on right now. And he needs to run, not walk."

THE MOORS ARE PURPLE WITH RAGE. Release their scent here. Every morning, before breakfast, Hilda sets out onto the moors with Florence and Violet, her sisters. Mia trails behind, listening in, figuring out how to be a woman in this big, imaginary space.

They walk with their different gaits and thighs and weaknesses. Heel twisting over the sty of the English countryside then out into the wide sky-earth with the soundtrack of their lives blurting out over the loudspeakers. This wide earth widening. This great plain spreading its fingers, incey-wincey into the darkest corners of their conversation. They talk about everything. They assess each problem in detail, consider their wifely responsibilities, laugh at the possibility of not caring, of affairs, of motel rooms in music video luxury. Mia's cleanly shaven seventeen year old legs flick stories at the wind, tales of their undoing, the soft creepiness of his mouthing beard, the strained readiness of his loins burning down this landscape, this world of promise. They talk about everything that is a problem and they solve nothing, just leave the sound of their voices clinging to the determined flora of The Moors.

They are old friends. They talk about running out into the landscape painting and not stopping. Land that they burn with their thoughts. All of it burning, warming up the earth, making mist that brings in knights, real men, that brings in steeds, real horses, that brings in England, my home. I weep for you like a nationalist at an Olympic football match. I chisel out my name. Hilda, on a rock. Hilda, on a tree. Hilda, out of sticks. Hilda, delivered in this delivery room that is rainy and sodden. She comes running at the camera, knackered, soaked through, splashed up the legs with mud.

"Here I am," she says.

Tale of the Small Green Weeds

VI

THE GREEN OF THE TREES HASN'T CHANGED, but something has, and if you left this place just like this, no cars, no people, for a few years, the whole place would be taken over by vegetation. This is the bottom of the ocean. Every city is Detroit.

There would be sound. It would come from every direction. Mostly it would come from the throats of birds and the wings of insects. Leaves would shiver and quiver their Tennyson song, only to be broken, mid-thrust, by Tanya Tagaq cracking and shunting revolution out of her body, spinning off the marble droplets of prophesy. She would sing the Vatican right off its feet, bring rats out dancing, spin pigeons of touristic fantasy over arches, under viaducts, trail choir boys by their tasseled locks over the soft socked feet of priests.

The odd piece of rubble or brick, dug at by ivy fingers, would drop on a bush—a light rustle—or onto cement—a click and then an echo.

And then eventually rock and stone would become sand, sand would find water, water would find whale, whale would find whirlpool, whirlpool would find whippoorwill, whippoorwill would find his daddy's switch and break it, daddy would make fire, fire would make industry, industry would make worker, worker would make brick, the third little pig would carry brick and it would make house, house would make sense of it all, fossil fuels would keep house warm, chimney would smoke, and the kid would scramble for her puffer and get back to square one. A fresh breath. A new start in an industrial wasteland waiting for the fuel to run out and the weeds to begin again their incessant quest for the sun.

Twenty-Eight

THE HUMIDITY MAKES VIOLET AND STEPHEN QUIET. They want to talk, but they can't be bothered to move their lips or activate their vocal chords. The silence, though, is unnerving. Violet wants not to care. She pretends she is in a movie, eclipsed by a soundtrack, shot from all angles, all busy and aesthetic, her head scarf fluttering at its tip, around the knot, like a bee at an anther.

Stephen can't stay away from her. They found this movie set on their way home from Hampstead Heath, where they made love like two men behind a bush.

The director, wearing jeans and a cowboy hat—they must be over from America—opens the door on a convertible, ladies first! and hands the key to Stephen.

"Why the glum faces? You're supposed to be in love," says the director. "Look like you are."

They set off from the set, followed by cars with cameras and camera men and grainy 1950s grains, and they don't really know what to say because they've been together for hours and have forgotten that Susan is watching Madame and Tom, and that Florence has been scheduled to peer through the net curtains in increments of three to five minutes. It's like they don't care anymore. They're done with worry. The storm is already dripping rain on the town. It will not slide past in the night. It will drench them. It will lure children to their windows where curtains magically dance in the glow of lightning wind. It's a metaphorical storm and it's a real storm and it's a storm in a book, but whichever way you look at it, it's a storm. And it's already here, even though this is a convertible and this is Rome circling back on us.

There they go now. Bill is forgotten here, not mentioned or thought about, his crowing, crying fingers on his face in a room lit only by streetlight. The rain has come now, hard, stinging pellets of water pooling on the leather backseat.

Stephen, the man driver, stops the car and rushes around to the lady's side. Violet is already out and running up the marble steps of a Piranesi etching—her wet toga clinging to her long, London-twiggy legs. She sits down, sheltered by the fact that *History Book* said this would happen and pats the step beside her.

"Sit."

"The car is getting drenched."

"Let it drown. We are at the bottom of the ocean already. Let it drown. Someone will rip out its entrails one day and turn it into a boat."

Violet looks up at Stephen with her most serious face.

"Will you come with me?"

"Where are you going?"

"Back to my quiet afternoon front room home where I die slowly, where strands of my hair can be found on every surface, where my children's ambitions crust over and explode."

"You make it sound so appealing." He pauses, looks out at the river of tourists surging past. "OK. I will come back with you, be with you, for one last month," Stephen says. "Then your obsession will fall from me like an x-ray apron and I will be faithful to Flo and she'll know exactly what happened, not through seeing, not through words, but through just because. And that's fine because she won't fuss. Occasionally she'll spill tea or coffee on her skirt and go ballistic and then cry herself into an exhausted heap, but she'll never accuse me of adultery or mention your name in this house again. Understood?"

"A month is all I need, Stephen. I'm almost crazy. A bit of a nudge and I'll be T.S. Eliot's wife—my dream occupation."

Really Violet is frightened by the prospect of all love coming to an end. No Bill. No Stephen.

Stephen is frightened by the fact that he stays because he doesn't know what else to do.

When did all this start? This mass of leavings. Standing around in hallways waiting for him to button up his coat, secure his feminine scarf; sneaking around on the landing looking through bars or peering out of windows as he drives away.

"Last night we kissed under a willow in a dream," says Violet, grabbing onto Stephen's hand of air, of nothing, as he pulls it away. "I called you back to me and put your hand on my right breast. Like so. You joked that it was small."

"Let's drive," he says.

They drive the winter road and he puts on music that he'd chosen earlier that day with her in mind. She cannot do herself up fast enough to resist the siren songs that shudder from the speakers.

They drive the winter road. She touches his hand on the gear stick. Her hand holds the halo of her wicked intent for minutes afterwards. The conscious looking and touching shakes open the shutters of her organs and meridians.

The hills are dusted with snow. Roadkill. A coyote or a dog. They are momentarily blinded by the sun.

STEPHEN DROPS VIOLET OFF OUTSIDE HER HOUSE. He knows it isn't time to "let out a huge sigh of relief" as he lets out a huge sigh of relief. The swooning Violet stumbles into the house and sits quietly before a dead fire. She reaches for the smelling salts; they peel off the black and white TV screen in their trembling celluloid splendour and drift quietly to the floor.

It's been this way for months, she thinks. I could see our mechanized winding down. He looked and then he regretted it immediately. Where has my beauty gone? This body was not the plan, the teenage fantasy. This body is not enough. This body has failed. My breath from the cum trees. My snail sadness, hotly misunderstood, hiding under the eiderdown.

VIOLET REALIZES, SADLY, that she will miss out on that bit with Bill when they fall in love again and start chasing each other around the house. Up and down stairs, spinning on banisters, loud, children loud, all over the walls and up the doors. Their old love split open to make room for new tentacles, feelers, antennae. That bit when they become creatures of the coral reef. Bright, succulent, bursting with life.

Twenty-Nine

MIA'S MOTHER IS ALL OVER THE FOOD, trailing it on the way to Mia's mouth, commenting on its sanity in this world that has gone to hell before its time.

"This food is not fit for human consumption," she warbles (because she is half-bird, half-woman) over the stacks of globally warmed TV dinners.

All the thinness of celery and radishes circles the radiant lumps of Mia's thighs that she hides under scrumptious skirts and leggy leggings. She is in the equivalent of Grade 12. Not sure how they do it in Italy, I put her in the requisite tartan skirt that shows her bum cheeks in a rain storm, muddy puddle water splashed up her long socks. I put her in an ironed shirt and a child's tie, smaller than a man's. One little tie passes one big tie. She feels the breeze of his pervert as he passes, but not at all because he is a businessman and the economy depends on businessmen and we need their sleeves-rolled-up hairy arms to steer us over the hard, parched soil. No rain. No rain for weeks, boss. *Shoot a fucking missile at those clouds!* the businessman scrawls on a piece of scrap paper that he finds in his glove compartment and shoves into his worker's hand.

She dresses as a stereotype and then sits there moving her peas from one side of the plate to the other. Little anorexic white girl, sack of bones in a white silk blouse, a gift from grandma who hasn't seen the finished product of Mia's body—naked or clothed—for years. The clothing almost makes it worse. Her shoes are clownish, never done up tight enough. Her eyes are big, as big as the fashion is. A fine layer of down covers her jaw line. *Lanugo*. Because Latin words take up entire sentences. Oh no, *lanugo*. It's a sign that things aren't right at home where mothers breathe fiery warnings along the necklines, waistlines, hemlines of their developing female offspring sprayed from the hip of a king, a god passing like a bird in flight past the window, showering his golden load over the girl's bones that want to protrude. For attention. For the love of Christ and nuns. For the snacks under the bed, twist-tied closed and stacked, shoved into backpacks, found under car seats on Sundays for dad days, crumbs like trails of whiskey breath on a husband dot the rec room, the den. Towers of saltines, bare and dry, crash into Mia's mouth, falling like the tumbling stacks of industry into the wallet of her father, who cuts ribbons and wages and then gets back to the office and a string of messages and responsibilities. The secretary has been there before and knows the signs on the girl who is over-confident in her bone-clacking splendour. Such beauty in nothingness, the poor child believes, spinning webs around her for warmth, snuggling up to daddy's arm in the elevator down to the parkade. Nobody can see me fluttering here, she thinks. I will escape through tiny cracks like a rabbit—warm, thick fur, but all bones in an emergency. *Lanugo* on the way we go.

MIA LEARNS TO EAT EVENTUALLY. Once she gets away from the clip-clip of her mother's hard words and into the beds of a few boys, struggling with their own versions of self-starvation, food starts to make sense in its sensual madness, its colourful wetness. Slowly she fills out into the flapper girl she becomes in this novel, with her red sequined dress taken from the wall of a vintage clothing store by a woman with Edgar Allen Poe style and a hooked pole. Mia's brown bob springs on the waves of male attention. She leans on arms, as before, but now not as a stick child. She is substantial, full of water and heat. Intentional.

But everything harkens back to that time of ticks being spat at her head over dinner. Clip. Clip. They fall from the table, lentils from the step-sisters' basket for her to pick up instead of going to the ball and getting chosen. And so she cannot help but check the labels of every single thing she eats, to weigh out the pros and cons of a chemical shitstorm that mommy said was on its way. To open the fridge in search of protein but finding none. Rummaging now to the back. Finding none. Going down to the town to buy some. Buying none. Turned off by everything that is wrong with everything that is wrong. Coming home with a bunch of carrots and some more cereal that she will eat with her fingers, without milk. Coming home and opening the fridge. Looking for protein, for iron. Finding none.

And then Jorgen comes into her life with his cult of promise and wants to pour gallons of milk down her throat, wants to rob every calf in the district of its shot of colostrum so he can build Mia's body from the ground up. He fattens her up for his bed, makes her his earth mother, rosy-cheeked Hilda replacement, pregnant with his child because Hilda cannot give him anything—just red water in the toilet bowl, monthly hysterics, and the quiet thinness of her knitting fingers making booties for other women's babies.

Thirty

BILL SHELTERS UNDER THE OVERPASS waiting for the rain to let up. There are burrs on his trousers—gorse, of course—and the spidery floss of dandelion wishes. He cowers like a rabbit that knows it has been caught.

England is all dual carriageways and roundabouts and pedestrian overpasses. Everything is so official and government approved. The countryside, space of roaming and love, has been sliced up into parcels, slit by bridal paths that hold walking trees at bay. Bill finds himself hiding out from progress on some leisurely concrete embankment carved out by the local council for no aesthetic reason whatsoever. The traffic zooms on by, soothing in its predictability.

Bill spots Hilda coming towards him, stumbling home from the doctor's house in her mud brown shoes. So lovely. So flaming against the dull sky.

She shimmies down the embankment in her MEC gear, hands sliding over shiny new rope.

"I'm thinking of adopting. Bringing in a new character," says Hilda.

"A baby?"

"No. An older kid. Maybe a child star. Fully trained, of course."

"Acting? Dancing? Singing? The whole gamut?"

"It would certainly come in handy in all this rain."

"What if it grows up to be stark raving mad?" asks Bill. "Will it turn your home into a zoo, a circus, a pantomime? Will it be a boy or a girl? Will you regret it?"

"Will I upset it?"

"Is it a rebound?"

"Handed up from the underground?"

"Will it be pretty? Too pretty?

"Will it be ugly? Too ugly?"

"Will it sleep with your wife?"

"My wife?"

"*My* wife."

"Are we still going with that story? What a classic! Jilted adopted brother pulls one over on the brother that was born down into the cud of the mother."

Bill is silent. He's pissed off and wants Hilda to shut up.

"Stephen could have kept it in his pants, I admit," says Hilda, feeling bad for being so insensitive.

Bill looks up at the sky. The rain doesn't seem to be going anywhere. He may have to make a run for the train station, holding Hilda's hand with one hand, the other holding a bone-dry newspaper to shelter their movie-laughing faces.

What do they have to laugh about?

Freedom. Their right to run out in it. Their right to sit tight under the overpass. Their right to love and be loved.

Hilda reads the last line, slides her arm around Bill's shoulder. "It's OK. Violet regrets it terribly. She still loves you, Bill."

VIOLET WASN'T YOUNG THEN. She was already a mother. Nothing was left to the imagination. She came "as is." She came out onto the landing and smiled down at Stephen with her eyes. Then she disappeared. He followed her into the back room. A room with tea chests and cardboard boxes stacked up against one wall, an unmade single bed against the other. She was already on the bed. Her housecoat was open, exposing her nude portrait.

But this is all in Bill's imagination. In mine. There probably were no smiling eyes filched from *Danny, Champion of the World* glistening over a yellow balloon.

Violet does not draw Jeremy Irons into some industrial bedroom. She is not the curtains that suggest suggestively. Nor is she the eyes in the mirror looking back into the room and making the man blush with excitement. She is in the land of silence, where concrete crumbles under the arabesques of ivy rootlets and drops, echoing, to the city streets below.

AND THEN SHE DISAPPEARS into the darkness of a block of flats in Hackney, wearing out the carpet with her slipper-shuffle, making origami from the beautiful gold foil of her cigarette packs.

Thirty-One

WHEN BILL LEAVES, Madame Bovary is happy to blame her father for everything. She follows Violet's lies like a puppy taken away from its mother too soon and then starts telling lies of her own. Tom is irritated by his sister, but he can't figure out why. His father has been up half of London, right? His father has abandoned them. It's not a good time. It never is. It's not a good time because mum is sick. Nothing the doctors can put a finger on but sick nonetheless. She's rarely out of the bed, although she does have moments of lightness and shrill joy that the children brace themselves for. They do not want to see her happy. It scares them.

This is the 1950s. Prams are everywhere. Lads are smoking on low walls with their legs stretched out, crossed at the ankles. Gays are keeping quiet about it. The working class is trying to raise their kids so they don't have to go to war while resenting them for not having to. Beehives are on their way. They will be devastating. They will smell of ashtrays and beauty parlour chemicals. Margate is in every photograph. The boys have soldier hair. The girls have ropes of golden locks stained black and white, waiting for someone to snap them with a Polaroid camera. Sometimes there are videos of children on bikes, mothers shooing away cameras while their shy eyes tell us about last night with the man behind the camera. He's been trying to make a cocktail that he picked up in one of those tropical places in the war. He forgets that the ice gave him a fever, diarrhea, a few days off to lie on his bunk with his eyes closed drifting in and out of England like a wave.

Violet wasn't sent to war. She worked in some factory in a short film you watched in high school History. She was smiling for the camera. Who wouldn't? Supporting our boys. Our men.

Her ambitions were never identified. There was nobody watching. Tom and Madame were too young to understand that mothers have dreams too, you know? They hugged her tightly whenever they could, only to feel her body become trunklike, sturdy but cold, her arms flat to her sides waiting to be taught how to flap and fuss around their darling backs. She was laughing and dying, hacking up phlegm that changed in colour from gross to worrying. Her lines had snapped as far as we were concerned. She came from some dark place and she returned there. Friendless. Husbandless. Free of dreams for far too many years.

BILL HAS BEEN GONE FOR LESS THAN A WEEK. Each day has been long, complicated, full of memory and meaning. Tom has counted the days and will continue to count them long after Bill is long gone. Church and State prevent his father from re-evaluating his choice to abandon his children. These war women are such a pain in the arse. They have so many demands. They've done everything wrong. "A woman gets lonely too," they say, as if what they say even matters.

But he wasn't at war. He was at the brewery working as a

carpenter. He worked there for forty years, he did. What did Stephen have to offer that he didn't? What part of the story is missing? It gets added and then added again, over and over, like making the house bigger for each new baby that is born. And it changes, the story changes, not just in the details but in the very foundation of its body. First it is a one-off. A motel room in America. Violet with the sheet pulled up to cover her breasts, Stephen coming out of the bathroom lighting a cigarette to find his brother a silhouette in the doorway. Then it is a long affair, passionate, movie-esque. Then it becomes the tragedy of the unrequited lover—sometimes Stephen, sometimes Violet, always crying. Then it becomes a lie in Bill's mouth to cover his own tracks as he skirts the department store looking for her face and bright red hair, her door mat that says WELCOME.

All that is left is Tom Sawyer and Madame Bovary being told lies. Occasionally an aunt tries to set things straight, but she does a bad job of it because she spends too long searching for euphemisms.

Thirty-Two

IT'S A SUNDAY. Sunny. All the families of London are out today. Violet has decided to take Tom and Madame for a picnic. She is tender in her choice of foods, even stopping to buy a bag of plums from the greengrocer's.

It takes three buses to get them where they want to go.

"It will be a long walk, but it will be worth it," says Violet as she sets off along a gravel path. Passing a lake they see swimming bodies flash white behind the rushes. Tom and Madame giggle together as friends, because they are, in that dark time of childhood when allies are crucial. Madame pushes her little brother into a laughing bush and he wings leaves at her, spinning out across the gravel.

Bill walks beside them, unseen, his body riddled with lies, holes shot through him to the sky behind, so blue, so bright, this fatherless Sunday.

"Hurry up, you two," calls Violet with her picnic basket swinging round to crash a party of nettles, dock leaves, found and tucked into Madame's sock for just in case. He fell, she said he fell right into a patch of nettles and writhed on the lawn like a frenzied wolf.

Bill wants to see how his children are getting on without

him. How the whore of his swollen love brings her brood up behind her like a train of flowers. Their laughter cuts to the quick and stings. He tears off into the woods and then cuts them off at the pass. Let us pass. Let us pass. Throw us heavy weights over the line between childhood and adulthood. Throw us, daddy. Pleeeease!

Tom walks through the ghost of his father like he is walking out onto the lake, where men pass underwater. Great looming pike. The fear is here, hanging off Tom's back, dragging him down and out of the afternoon that is supposed to be so good, such good times, that he must etch into his memory cave to revisit when all there is is Violet hanging over the toilet bowl, her crown of cancer fallen beside her like a wet towel. This will not be it, he cries down into his own throat because there are no words for this father-love rising up inside him with its fullness and magic.

"Come back," Tom whispers. "Guide me through this maze of poverty with my eyes open.. And the priest. Guide me past the priest and his flapping black cloth. And the car that spins on the wet road. Guide me past that. I can take your hand, daddy. I can take your hand and come with you, wherever you're going."

IN THE SHADE OF A GLADE Violet stands behind the billowing picnic blanket in a photograph that Madame takes with her make-believe camera. Tom runs off to the lake, tosses a rock at the back of a man, surfacing to spit water from his bearded D.H. Lawrence mouth.

Tale of the Small Green Weeds

VII

THE FOOD BANK FEELS THE THUD of another can of out-of-date beans and wieners.

Two figures are sharing a ripe fig. In the root of the alley they dig around in the remains of a woman's sushi lunch, fight over a pizza slice. One is celiac and knows that his belly will rise like dough into the meal that the gift horse has given them.

The supermarket extends over great surfaces, its metal shelves stocked and restocked into pans of boiling water, into recipes and locked dumpsters and landfills. Unpronounceable ingredients quiver from the mouths of amateur chefs into the ears of supermarket staff that know this maze of excess off by heart.

The TV has us gorging radicals finding things to do with offal and squab. We pat ourselves on the back, then scoop off the scum that films our materialism so we can deliver it proudly, on the verge of tears—*I must be PMS-ing!*—to the food bank.

We continue to drive through the figures' territory with our trunks full of reusable shopping bags stuffed with groceries. Cupcakes, for a treat, nestled in their waxy shells. Vacuum-packed pizza crusts, tetra-packed juice, migrant-worker-packed anti-oxidant berries. Child buckled snuggly into the most recently approved car seat (unapproved one leaning against the back fence biodegrading in the rain).

Thirty-Three

JUST BEFORE BILL LEAVES FOR GOOD, the family takes a holiday. They go to the coast, of course, and find everything waiting for them with their name on it. The days of pampering the consumer have just begun and this family is out on the sands riding donkeys to prove it.

Sitting on their towels, the four of them lined up, picture perfectly, they listen to the waves seething in along the beach, sucking the tide out to sea. They will not need to scramble up the sands, carrying baskets and parasols and Parisian *choux* pastry. For now, they are listening to the waves and the breeze that deceptively cuts the heat of the sun and flutters anything fluttery—including a ribbon of fluorescent plastic, not yet invented, that graces the turret of a sand castle.

Bill and Violet don't touch. They're done with that. Two kids later and they're done with making them. In their minds they might be tender, on the sand, early evening, nobody around, just the waves and the gulls. But in this living room here they keep to their towel territories, occasionally responding to a question from one of their children, or sitting up on their elbows to look at bodies moving across the sand. There are crisscross patterns of footprints that the breeze fiddles away. Far up the beach, near the road, is barbed wire, lost and looking for Germans on the horizon.

Ferris wheel somewhere. Music twanging out of a tin box, candy floss eating into the enamel of Piranesi's figures' teeth at the rate of a glass of Coke experiment. The cavity draws solace from the dentine, retreats into the bone, a burrow, a warren of rot.

The teenager running the donkey rides has big lips. They are half wet by his mouth, half dried by the sun. The line is strict between the two segments. A girl is leaning in her white, tight shorts against a flagpole. She clicks her ring against the metal. A mating song. She is not afraid of boys.

"You're blocking my view," says Madame to her brother, who is simply standing to change into his swim shorts, not, as she believes, trying to ruin her chances of finding a husband. In a few days Madame Bovary will climb onto a train with her brother and parents and return to London where she will pose before her dressing table mirror as a conduit for Elizabeth Taylor in a Steinbeck paragraph. James Dean will hover outside the window, kicking random stones to nowhere, his eyes shifty and remote.

HOURS INTO THEIR HOLIDAY Violet is already thinking about Stephen. Bill hasn't walked in on them yet. He hasn't turned the door knob and walked into the motel room. He's done no such thing. He will though, in less than a month. She thinks about calling Stephen from a phone booth, but can't think of an excuse to give Bill and then Flo, if she answers the phone. What would she say anyway? I miss you? Even though I am not your wife. Stupid woman. She wants to thump the side of her head over and over, but there is no private place to do that crazy thing. Their holiday chalet is open plan, American style. Everybody watching everybody else's sunburnt flesh. Mothers get to cook while simultaneously joining in with the political discussion being had by their men's pipe smoke. Children have nowhere to hide the sex in their fingers. The adults can hear the children breathing while they fight and drink and climb all over one another in the living room. Children that aren't asleep can hear the sarcasm in their parents' voices without knowing what sarcasm is. Everything is a joke that isn't funny.

Violet must decide how she is going to get through the next four days. Bill is being his usual vacant, smiling self. Occasionally, he gets pissed off at the kids for getting sand in the wrong places, or wetting his legs with their seaweed whips, but mostly he is agreeable and jolly.

VIOLET FLICKS A BROKEN PIECE OF SHELL off her ankle and pushes up the brim of her hat. She can see Madame with her toes in the surf, Bill chasing Tom Sawyer across the wavy sand still wet from high tide. Their feet make the slap-slap sound of masturbation. Tom dodges Bill in his imp body, gets away, and goes charging through the shallow water until he falls laughing, splashing his sister in her quiet romance of men, fresh from war, falling into the frothy water at her feet.

"Bill!" Violet calls from her towel, waving her hand widely through the air.

Bill turns and jogs across the sand to her. "Yeah?"

"Do you love me?"

He turns away from Violet and watches his children now playing together in the shallows. He hates this question.

"Answer me. Do you love me?"

"Violet . . . "

"You can't, can you? You never can. Oh, bugger off!"

Bill begins walking back across the sand to join his children. Violet throws a pebble that hits him on the back of the head. She throws it too hard, too late. As it flies out of her hand she regrets the day that pebble came into her life.

"Ow! Fuck. Violet! What on earth!?"

She has covered her mouth with both hands, tight, and is up and facing him, straddling her towel to keep the sand off.

"I am *so* sorry, Bill. I didn't mean for it to hit you. Ow! What the hell?" Violet is rubbing her cheek. She looks down at the pebble that Bill has just thrown at her. It is larger, more menacing. "I didn't mean to hit you," she cries out, too loudly. Someone on a nearby towel is now listening in. Bill throws another one. It clips her on the side of the head this time. She is too shocked to duck. Her heart is racing. She is frightened. He picks up another and twists his arm back as if he is about to skim a stone across the calm sea of their first date. It hits her on her left thigh. Stings. Draws blood.

This scene has the potential to turn really nasty—a husband and wife lobbing stones at each other until one or both of them end up dead or in the hospital. It could be a scene of wife-battery, public, jolly, a man chasing his wife over the beach in fast motion, both of them spraying sand in people's faces and open Tupperware, him aiming for her head. It could be her, towering over his blood-smudged, sunburnt body, holding a large barnacled rock that she is about to drop right on his face.

But it will stop here. 3–1 to Bill. Violet daren't provoke him more than she already has. He is walking back to the sea. Once he reaches the water he keeps walking, striding through the shallow waves until the water is up to his hips. Then he's off out into the clouded grey channel, away from his family. Tom Sawyer stands on the beach watching Bill swim away. After a while he starts to wonder when his dad is going to turn around and swim back, whether he'll get tired and start clutching his chest like Wally did when he died. He looks back at his mum. She is lying on her stomach shaking quietly. Crying again, Tom thinks. He looks at Madame Bovary who has hauled a dressing table and full length mirror down to the water's edge. She is holding scarves and necklaces up to her neck and turning her head from side to side so that she can be all men from all angles. He looks out to sea and sees his father treading water, looking out at the horizon; in a moment Bill flips down under the waves. When he surfaces he begins to swim on his back towards his son, his daughter, his wife. Tom Sawyer decides to swim out to him with a raft he has built in his imagination. Just in case. Heart.

VIOLET'S SHOCK AT BILL'S BEHAVIOUR gives way to anger and then apathy. Before she even gets around to arguing with him, she has made up her mind to plant clues to her affair with Stephen. The beach is strewn with items of her clothing. Moving from outer garments to inner ones, Bill gathers his wife's clothes and arranges them into the shape of her. Suddenly she steps out from behind a screen, planted surrealistically on the distant beach. She is naked.

Her eye zooms in on the shirt that Bill is pulling over his damp skin. The button is there. Sewn on with the wrong coloured thread, but there. Doing its job.

Thirty-Four

STEPHEN AND FLORENCE AND THEIR KIDS and pregnancy arrive at the beach after Bill and Violet have been there for two days. Stephen and Violet did try to synchronize their four-day family holiday, but both Bill and Flo said that two days would be enough. Once Bill and Violet return to London, Stephen and Florence will have two days alone. To fight.

ALL THE COUPLES ARE DOING THIS YEAR IS FIGHTING. It's the in thing. Over in Germany Hilda and Jorgen are raging up and down the hallways of their invaded home. Mia is a statue of *libertad*. She enters rooms only to have to duck to avoid ash-trays swishing ashily past her head. She always comes alone. A model in a studio. A cousin in a steamy kitchen. A long-socked flapper girl after a bath. The house begins to smell of her.

There were so many years of harmony. Every couple turned into an album cover. Coney Island graphic design. Madonna on a fence. The honeymoon became a vial of honey. She breaks it during a nervous breakdown. He breaks it like an addict. The honey becomes familiar, old hat. The addict sucks at the tube.

There are those who come in couples—usually temporary, usually fleetingly fond of one another—and there are those who come alone. The guests at the party part to let Mia through. Nobody will like her dress five years from now, but this year it is gorgeous. Polyester before it is invented.

As the night wears on, Mia is with most of the husbands at the party. After a while, she keeps her dress up around her waist, waits in the darkness of the "may I take your coat?" bed, feeling buttons and zippers and bristly material bother the bare skin on her bum and legs. Later, as the wives are coated by their husbands, they pull out handkerchiefs and baby wipes and lipstick-blotted tissues to fiddle with the wet patches on their lapels and sleeves. Oh Frank, they say. Oh Nigel. Be more careful next time. Mia is still lying on the bed; the guests shove her over gently as they search for their coats. She smokes, tapping the ash off her cigarette into the broken-then-glued-back-together ashtray perched on her sternum.

THE COUPLE HAS NO TIME FOR THE SINGLE. They never invite her. She is new currency looking to exile old.

Here we have two couples. Four children. One pregnancy. For Flo this is the worst of the three. She's worn out and angry that she's pregnant. What was she thinking? Hilda, meanwhile, is picking red debris from the toilet bowl to examine it. Nobody is ever happy.

They congregate in Stephen and Florence's chalet because that's where the liquor is. Bill barely drinks—a pint here and there—but Stephen is in love with the fumes as they seep into his nostrils, are drawn into his throat and belly. He's the one that is up at the wet bar tinkling out the music of ice on glass. "What'll it be, brother?"

"I'll have whatever you're making."

"Me too," says Violet.

"Want a Guinness, love?" Stephen asks Florence.

"Sure, why not?"

Florence is watching Stephen jigging around like a cricket making happiness out of horror. Violet tries to catch his eye. Hers are smiling. His are too. Bill is looking out the window watching the children play badminton. He'd rather be out there with them.

"Have you had fun so far, Bill?" asks Florence.

"Oh, sure. It's lovely here. Lovely."

Within a few hours they are dancing around the chalet, switching partners, switching back jealously, cracking jokes against the rim of the music. The children are sitting around the radio, twiddling the knob now and then, fighting over which songs are good for dancing. They sneak sips of Florence's Guinness, steal the umbrellas from finished cocktails, suck on ice that tastes of rum and tinned pineapple juice. Eventually the children are sent out to buy fish and chips, which they begin eating on their way back to the chalet, a beacon on the hill, the adults overseeing the world below.

IN THE EVENING, after wasting time trying to string up a ripped badminton net between too-far-apart trees, the group heads down to the beach. Florence and Violet stumble over tree roots, hold each other up, laugh about wetting themselves. The children scramble down the edge of a chalky slope, imagining a rock slide in the Alps, the nimble bone-hard legs of goats inside their own. Momentum spits them out onto the dark, tree shaded road below the holiday park with their canvas shoes slapping the asphalt.

Flo has fallen in her laughing piss into the shivering soil. Seriousness descends upon her muddied dress, the only nice one she has that doesn't make her look like a whale with legs. Violet dusts her off and shouts at the men that this is not good for the baby and then she finds a bench for Florence to sit on and they wait there while the men and children head off to find crabs and shells and seaweed necklaces and wigs.

Thirty-Five

BY THE TIME THEY GET BACK TO THE CHALET Hilda and Jorgen have arrived from Germany. Their bikes are leaning against the side of the chalet, tent poles and pegs strewn across the badminton area, a canvas tent spread out to air. There aren't enough fish and chips left over so the children are sent out for more. They run off down the hill whooping, money sweating in Madame Bovary's responsible palm.

Hilda sees that Florence is pregnant. She immediately regrets coming. She's only here for Jorgen. He feels that he has been given a flat role that completely eclipses the creative genes he inherited from his mother, whose stories swarmed around his head like snowbees. He remembers that the sheets drying on the line that Frau German Surname described had a scent, a texture, a distinct thwacking song. He was in Heidelberg. She was in Stuttgart. He opened the letter and her washing line fell out into his lap. Gentle and full of kindness, she raised Jorgen to be warm to all strangers. Mia was a stranger. She was placed in his kitchen, a doll model in a black dress and white apron, cheeks flushed with paint and varnish, a nut of a head knocking against the china cabinets. She had come all the way from Italy, alone, a young woman vulnerable to a new tongue, to the taste of strangers. Everything about her delighted him, but that doesn't mean he slept with her. He didn't. Ever. He didn't even touch her, unless you count shaking her hand at the train station, guiding her out of the path of some stinging nettles, or shielding her from the neighbour's temperamental dog.

Mia was brave to flee *The Italian Saga*. It was too long from the beginning. Right from the get-go it had too many characters. There was no telling when it would end or how many dramas would spill their bloody cargo over her painted-on shoes. Women with flouncing bosoms and manly voices kept thickening the plot with their stir-y spoons; bespectacled men with political aspirations kept rolling up their sleeves and drinking small glasses of red wine with their kissy lips. She was needed to fill a marriage to somebody from a well to-do family. The feast was established. The musicians booked. It was either become the wife of a landowner and walk about with a parasol for eternity or run away.

Getting out of a novel isn't easy. It requires gumption and style. It requires ironing out the kinks in your character so that you can leave her in place, the husk of your being, without drawing attention to the fact that the inner workings are missing. She still passes as a character—none but the sharpest of readers notice that she is gone—but she is forgotten easily, never becoming the subject of term papers or conference presentations. "Oh, Mia. I forgot about her. You're right. She *does* marry Giovanni. I guess that makes her an important character." Or: "Oh, Mia. I never remember her. She doesn't really leave an impression on me."

Of course she doesn't! She's not there.

She's in Germany. In Heidelberg. Her apartment in Rome has been let to two girls from France who invite Italian boys back at night, Catholic-style. Her mother has found other characters to plague with insults and criticisms. She doesn't even notice that her daughter is only a husk of her former self, even when the husk rustles on dry August afternoons, even then.

TODAY MIA HAS DECIDED to work as a chambermaid at a holiday camp in Margate. Just because. Our couples see her coming. Hilda puts down her bag of tent pegs and runs into the house to warn the others. "Be nice," threatens Jorgen, pointing at Hilda with firm eyeballs. "Be nice."

"Need any sheets or towels," Mia calls through the open door. She can see the plates covered with half eaten portions of fish and chips. There are glasses on every available surface. The tall man is drunk. She has seen him down by the pool cursing the pop machine. He speaks to her in his tall voice, asks for a stack of towels, no sheets.

"Can I get your dirty ones then?"

He stumbles off loudly to the bathroom to collect the towels. The women stare at her wooden body and wonder how she keeps it so freshly varnished. Violet looks her up and down as a kind of warning.

The children enter the chalet loudly, squeezing past Mia as she stuffs the dirty towels into a white sack. Tom Sawyer looks up at her, slyly. She's seen him in the pool trying to hold his sister under water, her shouts of panic echoing through the chlorine and music. Canned. Chemical. On holiday time. When Madame Bovary surfaces her face is arsenic white. But she can do that. It's her party trick. Black sludge spills from her mouth out onto the pool deck.

"Don't worry," says Mia. "I'll clean it up."

Thirty-Six

HILDA KEEPS HER DISTANCE from Florence all evening. She sits close to Jorgen, holding on to his arm like an anxious child. She doesn't want to be sitting here with these strange English people who have their own ways of doing things, but she promised Jorgen that she would come with him to the green room and help him fix whatever needed fixing.

Jorgen is talking to the men in the room, even though the women are right there listening in—tassels at the edge of discourse—giving their two bits.

"I'm a stereotype," he says. "I don't talk very much, most likely because I have so many secrets."

"Like what?" asks Bill.

"Like my affair with Mia, like my previous relationship that ended because I was violent."

"Were you?"

"No, I wasn't"

"Then why did Hannah say that you were?"

"Beats me. My theory is that she hates men."

There is a hush in the room. Even the children stop what they are doing and look over at the adults.

"You think so?" asks Stephen. "She's been pretty good to me."

"You're having an affair."

Violet looks at the ground. Florence flinches in her seat, gets up, goes to the sliding door and looks out across the holiday park.

"Well, so is Violet," says Stephen, defensively. "And Bill, don't you get one over on Hilda when she's working at that department store?"

"I think so. Haven't read my lines for a while, but that does ring a bell."

"See. That's most of us."

"All of us," corrects Florence.

"You too?" asks Hilda. "Who with?"

"I'm not sure. I just feel it coming. I feel him coming . . . Oh look! There he is. He's coming up the hill right now."

Everyone gets up and goes over to the chalet door. The children even step outside and walk forward to meet the man. He's very handsome. Florence deserves that. He's a rescuer type and carries a coil of rope over his right shoulder as a sign of his best foot forward.

Madame Bovary greets him with enthusiasm. "Welcome to our humble chalet. I take it you are here to liberate Florence from her cracking marriage? Florence is the one in the checkered skirt. She's awfully nice."

Everyone cheers.

Stephen cheers because it says "Everyone cheers," but inside he wants to do anything but cheer. He doesn't want Florence to be with another man, especially one graced with the rope of rodeos and mountaineering. He wants to cry, but that isn't manly, even after seven rum and pineapples, even though he strode in George Orwell's body through the thrumming grasslands, confident in his sex.

BUT THIS IS WHAT HAPPENED. It's all true. There was an adopted brother with a name that may or may not have begun with S. Violet was on top. The door was open. Nobody was expected. That day there was an explosion at the brewery and everyone was sent home early. Bill hadn't even opened his lunch, so he sat on a bench on the way home to eat it. As he ate he thought about overpopulation and exhaust from more and more buses and lorries and cars. By the time he got to the last bite of his sandwich his lungs were black and in need of a canary to light the way out. Even with stopping on the bench for lunch he arrived home four hours early. They had just finished. Violet had put her underwear back on but she was barechested and wet around the eyes from laughing. Stephen was completely naked with the sheet and blanket pulled up messily around his lower legs. His eyes happy, too.

At the moment Bill entered the room, Violet had just retrieved her lit cigarette from the ashtray on the night table. It wasn't a motel, but it had that feel. The children were both at school. The alarm clock ticked through the silence of the moment of discovery. Violet did not attempt to cover her breasts. Stephen did not leap up and dive out the window into *The Canterbury Tales*. It was just a scene. In anyone's life, in anyone's throat of sorrow.

Bill closed the door and just stood there staring at a chip in the yellow paint. After a few moments, aware of the sounds of the two of them rustling up a couple of outfits, he moved towards the bathroom, stopped, turned around and walked down the stairs and out of the house. He forgot to put on his shoes so he slipped into his wellington boots, which he kept in a cupboard outside the front door. The inner skin of the boots felt cold and dry against his feet. He walked miles that day, through the meadows of Paradise, past the cork trees of

Montseny, through the sound of cow bells *ting-ting-ting*-ing in the mountains, down to the River Thames. Great river of many voices. Great glistening river of pre-industrial utopia. By the end of the day, Bill was a little farther south, where there were women to be had in public houses, and the rent had already been squared away on a small room that had nothing added to it but a pair of wellington boots, a wallet, and a wrist watch.

HE WILL EVENTUALLY SURPRISE US ALL. He is a man, but no matter. They are men, but no worries. Take these women to be your lawful wedded ones. Wrap them in cartoon dreams come true and then say men are good guys, good solid good guys.

Bill, you have the rest of this book to prove yourself. Or will you try to tongue-kiss me in your council house? Will you?

Stephen? Jorgen? Challenge me. Prove me wrong.

Violet? Hilda? Florence? What do you have to say for yourselves? Are you blowing smoke into your children's faces? Are you weeping uncontrollably on a monthly basis? Are you turning a blind eye to the cries at the gates of your fortresses? What are you doing to grow them up right?

I took you for a hefty bunch of characters. You pushed out my babies, one by one, with your pokey brooms, women, your pokey rakes, men. You took over this space and lorded it over us all and you said, "Look at me in my Drama Dressing Gown! Look at me flowing down the stairs like an apparition at the mercy of a fast-forward button!"

You took over my parlour with your conversations, my bedroom with your fucking and your fucking up, and my kitchen with your meat-heavy dinners. You took up all my free white space with your large egos and your dastardly melodramas. Out went the Grand Tour and its postcard mania! Out went the underdogs! Out went the babes of historical fiction! Exiled to an eternal Ferris wheel ride.

THE FERRIS WHEEL HAS CLOSED FOR THE NIGHT. The doctor's field trip of artists is down in the sand, in the dark, with the wind pouring in over the crest of the channel. The figures find their feet rooting for wet sand, nesting.

"Why has she brought us here?" asks one of the men, twisting around to see a whole group of their folk scrambling up a wall and sprinting off down the promenade.

"Where are they off to? Are they ever coming back?"

The figures are looking out to sea. In the dark you can make out their outlines. Some have hair that is long, fluttering in the wind, flapping at their faces like the hands of babies. They ignore the distraction. Others are cold and dreaming of beds they don't have, hugging their knees to their bodies, squeezing them as close as they can get. "Has *Vedute di Roma* even started yet? That might be where the others are off to. Should we follow them?"

Without answering, one of the figures stands up. He heads off in the direction of the promenade, stumbling a little in the sand.

The rest of the figures get up and follow him. Wikipedia shudders briefly in her ever shifting skin. The landscape that is Margate lifts in the wind, a sheet of plastic, casting characters at their bodies like crumbs at a visit of birds.

THERE'S NOTHING TO WORRY ABOUT. Before the tourists arrive, even those early-bird types, the whole scene will be raked over and forgotten.

Tale of the Small Green Weeds

VIII

THEY NAME THE OPERATION AFTER JUPITER, although he was ornery and horny and, at times, horned, to cover the fascist—or is fascist too smooth of a word, as in "my fascist grandfather always made us wipe the mud off our shoes"?—sweeping up of the little people in the streets. Migrant workers. Asylum seekers. The poor. The hatred and fear has gotten into every tunnel in the warren. We thump out the disaster, fuck each other, and then kill our misfits in the womb. We tear out across the meadow in delight only to be stopped short at the fence of chicken wire that confines us to our beastly bodies and our bodily beastliness.

Piranesi's beggar leaning on a stick is stopped by the police. Clothes maketh the legal citizen, not the man. His brown skin is not the result of two weeks on the Riviera. His two young daughters peep out from behind him like cuckoos on the hour. He is plagued by the awkwardness of not belonging, the terror of having daughters that may or may not reach the promised landscape. Of debt. Of bad boyfriends. Of prejudicial policies and bureaucrats in wide cravats. The daughters spread out in search of wages and husbands. Their fragile religions fluttering in the wind.

THE MEDITERRANEAN COAST cradles the graves of waves then rises flatly into its plains and groves. Tourists form creeks that swell to rivers, tracking the clustering hoard of *in situ* artifacts and crumbling walls. Leaned against, shot sweating against, etched on a postcard. Sucking the flea-bitten teats of city wolves, our Mars babies grow to be men, one stronger and greedier than the other. The city is founded on the notion that it will grow quietly and in its own time, like a fetus, until it is known to all as the warehouse of clutter and junk.

Nobody can live comfortably in and among all this crumbling. The world hoards its expensive cargo, hauls it into museums and vaults and libraries. Grudgingly permits it to go off on tours. The artists prefer to drape waif-like material over objects that are made of plastic than to etch out the grains and slivers of a silver plate.

Piranesi shudders and goes back to his obsessive cataloguing of human folly.

THE CITY'S POLICE FORCE is made up of men and women who have their own stories full of closets. They hear the talk, though. They hear the talk and know that someone must be scapegoated and interned indefinitely pending the proper documentation. The human rights activists buzz around the entrances of police stations with their phones set to camera mode. They see the usual: History is too cluttered to teach us anything. They hear the usual: We might get hungry. We might get hungry. The last one here has to leave.

Thirty-Seven

TODAY THE CHARACTERS WILL HEAD BACK to their novel-houses in their novel-countries that have not been researched, except for a month of flipping through the pages of a coffee table art book, purchased on a trip to Montserrat.

The smokestacks are cold, but the thought is what counts. The government-sanctioned and -operated sterilization programs have stopped, but the same genocide goes on in the family planning of wasp women and their businessmen husbands. "I don't want something with extra fingers and toes coming out of me!" Oh, but it will; it will. It will come out whether you like it or not. The monster dreams in the last trimester will come true just as the apple tree spawns another bumpy apple. Mother tree calls to the wind to shake it down to the ground where the geese will devour its mealy heart. Mother tree calls to the farmer to shake his stick in among her leaves to draw out the weak one, splinter it off from the bushel. She is so embarrassed.

Hilda is frightened that her child will be feebleminded and webfingered and harelipped. Jorgen is quietly desperate. On holiday, he spends time observing Florence the earth mother tend her brood of nameless children, her gentle voice curled around their little heads, caressing them ever so quietly, while the adults drink and dance and flirt with one another. When the children cannot fall asleep—it is nobody's fault, there is too much noise—she is the one that climbs up the ladder into the loft to lie down beside them and hum a lullaby. She is the one to pour a glass of water for Madame and pass it up the ladder. Jorgen watches her and is moved. Oh *maman,* why did you have to die in the first line of a novel? Oh *maman,* why wouldn't I look at you in your coffin? I regret that now. I dream of unscrewing the lid and lifting it and seeing you there perfectly dead. Beautiful. It wouldn't have hurt to look at you, *maman.* What a dog I am!

Jorgen feels Hilda pushing her nails into his bare arms, clinging on, desperate for a cigarette but knowing what will happen to Violet, the wrinkles already setting around her mouth and on her forehead. Hilda would like to go out to the tent now, listen to Jorgen pissing against a bush—How loud!—then curl into him, spoon him like a bosom friend before turning away and feeling the tent breathe against her mouth.

In the morning heat, she will unzip the tent, slide her bedhead against its damp inner membrane, bend her stiff forty-something back and emerge into the bright, sweet-smelling morning of the campground. There, on a camping chair she will see Florence sitting with her back to the chalet, wide awake with her hand circling her belly, baby kicking good morning from within. Nobody sterilized, nobody empty of all promise.

Hilda can't enjoy a conversation with a mother, even her own, who she sent to a nursing home because the sun was in her eyes—there is no God—and who she visits only on set dates, prearranged and encouraged by the directress of the home and written in black pen on Hilda's calendar as MOTHER.

The women at work all have children and they all talk about them in the lunch room. Hilda hears that the baby walked his brother's pajamas down the hallway light on through the sister's first bra bicycle wheel stuck in the mud; hears the three trimesters puking out the car window on the way to the first shots; notices the pre-pregnancy bulge in the woman she hopes is just getting fat. The announcement! The announcement! The baby shower cake invites that bring her into twenty-first century North America riding a donkey for the plodding slug of preordained clotted blood. She must rest assured that the women's "ooo" and "aaa" cacophony will not stain her. Statuette. Majorette. Period-free. Held back by plastic wrap. The little cotton sandwich held in place by the panting vinyl skirt.

There is nobody to blame. Hilda is so beautiful and noble. She flashes the trees and bushes with her beauty, finds boyfriends lurking in crevices happy to take her back. And then they move on, find wives, have baby, have baby, have baby, and the photos pour in, slap against the windows and stay there. This one was at Christmas when she was only a year old. This one was when he hadn't slept properly for days and then got inside a cardboard box and put a colander on his head. This is peace in daddy's hairy bear arms, a breeze stealing up the porch steps. This is pretending to smoke granddad's pipe. This is snow. This is laughter. This is the terror of the cuteness of baby clothes.

She turns her back on the gaggle of nurses sharing a photograph of someone's newborn and stirs her tea until the teabag breaks and black grinds ruin the milky brown smoothness of her mid-morning break.

"Hilda, take a look at this cutie," a nurse calls from across the room.

Hilda remains stirring the tea, lost in thoughts of all her losses over the years and how she will make it work this time; this time will be the right time. She saw a double rainbow yesterday. A sign, surely. An omen of what good is about to come. Twins?

"Hilda! Hilda, come see this."

Keeping her back to the women in the centre of the staff room she turns towards the door, ESCAPE ROUTE, and holding her cup of tea as if it were a precious gift she walks slowly, pointing one toe forward and down, the next toe forward and down, a five-year-old self-conscious before a group of relatives who clap enthusiastically at her quiet show of nothing ballet.

The nurses go back to their cooing. They're used to madness around here.

Once outside the staffroom, Hilda runs—yes, with a cup of sloshing tea—to the office and slams the door. Behind her a trail of grainy splashes spells no regret. She presses her back against the office door and cries. She doesn't care how loudly. Her body shakes, rattling the door handle like she is trying to get in. Let me in! Let me into your clubhouse of baby powder and onesies!

Dr. Grebing is in the office. He's standing over by the art drawers, turned to her, embarrassed, trying to shuffle drawings loudly enough to make her look up.

It works. She stops in her sobbing tracks and stares at the doctor.

"Fuck you!" is the best she can come up with. "What are you looking at?!"

The doctor turns to the chest of drawers and commences sorting papers that are already sorted.

"I . . ."

"Don't."

"I . . ."

"Don't!" Hilda throws her cup across the room, not hard, but hard enough to get him to stop. It breaks in two.

They both move to pick up the pieces. He picks up one. She takes the other. They look at each other for a moment. And then, First Position. The music begins. First they dip into the centre, find a starting point—the bonding of the two halves of a broken cup. Perfect, but for the crack that will show and harbour germs. They pull their halves away and dance back into their own private spaces, put their pieces down so their hands are free. And now they are dancing. Hands together, bodies closer, then apart, her away, her returning, him behind, her in front, her in hiding, him in finding, her an erupting shadow in her uniform that is too tight. She removes it. Her slip is slippery and loose. She springs up, sinks down into her bent knees, his strong arms lifting her because she is light, not pregnant, a springing youth with oiled joints swallowed by a Kate Bush video.

They are out of breath. Smiling.

Hilda pulls her uniform back on, retrieves the two halves of the cup and drops them into the bin, and then she kisses the doctor on the cheek.

"I love you," she says.

Thirty-Eight

HILDA IS IN THE CAMPGROUND TOILETS. Sad place to be, even on a good day. She looks hard at the swipe on the toilet paper. Pink. That warning pink that tells you not to meet your gorgeous friends at the swimming pool. That spiteful pink that tells you there'll be one more month of waiting. And some. She drops the evidence into the toilet and flushes. There's an entire day ahead of her before she can cry on Jorgen's chest in bed.

When she comes out of the stall she sees Florence brushing her pheasant long hair at the sink. Hair you want to touch and wrap around your face.

"You have such beautiful hair. Can I touch it?"

Florence crinkles up her nose ever so slightly. "Sure."

Hilda used to get her younger sister to lie across her lap and spread her hair out over the couch cushion like a fan. She would pick and fuss at it for ages, longer if her sister moved, which she invariably did, until she had a perfect fan with strands going out in perfect straight lines. Once her work was done she would always tell her sister to turn around and take a look, which made them laugh. "Seriously! Take a look. Your hair is huge!"

Her sister has been dead for over ten years now. She killed herself in the footnote of somebody else's story. Nobody made a big deal about it because the accident that killed her three girlfriends took up a larger space in the newspaper of people's imaginations. The girls had known that the cliff edge was unsafe. They had known not to go near it. She had shouted to them from the path, her perfectly straight blonde hair whipping about her in the autumn wind, rising even then to a higher pitch as if singing a warning to the girls; her wooden pin legs stuck deep in the mud of the path so that even after the ground gave way and the girls fell screaming to the rocks below she didn't move a muscle, just stood there with her mouth wide open and her hair still at it.

HILDA REACHES OUT HER HAND and runs it slowly down the full-length memory of her sister's hair. She does it a second time. This time with her eyes closed.

"Thank you," she says, holding back her tears, feeling her cramps starting. "It's exactly like my sister's hair."

ALTHOUGH THE DESERT OF HILDA'S BODY lay parched in the face of onlookers, underneath there swirls a great ocean of life in the cool sand. The yolk of lizard eggs suggests water. Cacti hint at the legs of teenage girls, the surge of their buds. In darkness, if you have the right pair of eyes, the desert becomes a veritable city of transition and escape, becomes the nocturnal secret of my hot hands pressed against the back of my man.

There in the cell of her body team ants, bats, eels, quail. Life. It bursts around us. Feather. It visits the palm of a child. Insect. It specks the windshield that flies down the motorway.

The wonder of a whole city of spring. Water, some ridiculous percentage of her body. It finds the ocean. We are all one. We rocks, we rivers, we lava, we lovers.

The replacement baby is a sheet of paper, a paintbrush, a glass of water, and a palette of watercolours. They weren't expensive. She makes baby after baby after baby in the quiet garden. Hangs them to dry on the washing line. This sadness must go.

Jorgen's sadness is quieter, more private. He notes the father angrily clipping the head of the child that came when money was tight, the unexpected child thrown into the air and barely caught. He listens to Mia's stories about the cruelty of her mother, puts on his coat and takes long, brooding walks until he is pronounced dead and gone. He returns after dark, comes in through the kitchen door so he can sneak up to the bedroom and sleep through the worry of his wife and lover. They discover him. Chastise him. Then bring him food, heavy blankets, bowls of things, bowls of things and water. Chestnuts, cold, but still royal food in the mouth of their man.

MIA IS YOUNG, a membrane intact, a second life. She is vessel and matter. Her room, the guest room, is right there, one unopened door away from creation. The baby appears in teacups and doodles, in stories and conversation. The baby boy is always potentially a girl, one whole 50 percent of him reserved for the princess cake. He is bud and chrysalis and drop of ejaculate on the head of the pin of angels. He makes women out of girls, is born with all the burning potential to overpopulate and pollute. He is resigned to love and hate, depression and ecstasy, peace and chaos. He is the tiny Jorgen absent from Hilda's womb.

Mia can do anything in this book or the next. She is prequel and sequel and idea. All dreams happen in order and with gusto. Her body is the flopping fantasy doll of anywhere. Chucked up on the pile of coats she is expected to be there when he gets back. The guest room is sparse, unfriendly; through the window she sees Hilda on a chair at the end of the garden that looks out over Lles de Cerdanya, cow bells convenient, Catalan elder rattling a rowan twig against the fence of some herd or other. She sees the vegetable garden glistening with water from an evening hose, nutrients crouched down waiting to spring goodness at the intestines of their gardeners.

Hilda is sketching something that she cannot see. She looks up from time to time but simply to rest her eyes. There is nothing worth observing that hasn't already been drawn or painted or sculpted by Art History. She is leafing through the patients' art work that she has committed to memory. There, lurking among the weeds and vines and black earth, are women with thighs on bikes, profiles of heads with noses that end up being appropriated by well-intentioned bohemians, inventions for people from other dimensions that do exist and are not figments or filaments or phantasmagorical wisps of the imagination. Hilda is part of it, that chain of creation, production, spent life, pain, love.

Mia sits at the edge of her bed dripping with High Priestess water. Her hands cling greedily to the cold iron bed frame; her future humped back lurks in her left shoulder doing nothing in particular; her eyes stream with tears. A little Jorgen grows quietly within. Baby that will be born from experience, birthed loudly between quiet swathes of relief, taken by the red-headed witch and raised on the softness of "yes" and "certainly, dear." She bakes the little loaf in the borrowed oven, feels it flip around in her soup of kindness and complicity. A gift from the author to the one who cries out to the gods, blood in the bowl an offering of voodoo goodness, a sacred tint, bright with the happiness of poppies or Japanese maple leaves cut through by the northern sun of a Canadian baby shower.

Back and neck aching, trying to carry too many things—paintbrushes, pad, glass of water, paint palette, bowl of grapes, tissue paper, twenty-first-century cell phone beeping incessantly at Hilda to get with the picture and get down to the fertility clinic—Hilda walks up to the house, tilting her head up to observe the upstairs windows where orphans with large eyes urge her to adopt them. She notes their grubby faces. She notes their FASD. One is a success story but there is no way of telling which one. All are lonely. All have been crying. All would stage the birth, slip out from behind the raised red cloth, and shout "Ta da!" while the family, here especially for the occasion, some coming from as far away as Hitler's Germany and Ford's Detroit, would clap enthusiastically, laughing bravo eyes at the new addition to the family.

Thirty-Nine

HILDA ARRIVES AT DR. GREBING'S OFFICE wearing the taut face of the insomniac. She doesn't know who else to tell. Jorgen has been gone every evening for over a week. Last night, she ate his dinner. She wasn't even hungry. She could see the appeal of a vegetarian diet as she bit into the ham of a pig's life body.

The doctor can see that Hilda is disturbed. "What's the matter? Are you OK?"

"I wouldn't normally ask anyone to help me, but I need help. Jorgen has traded in his character for a glazed-eyed, dribbling cult follower. I need you to help me snap him back into reality."

"Does he want to be snapped?"

"No. Of course not. But I need him back. I need him to be him again. I know I've been spending a lot of time with you, and with Bill, but Jorgen's my husband and there's decorum and tradition and sickness and health at stake here. I even baked a cake for him. With his name on it."

FOR THE SAKE OF MY FEAR and hatred of soft and luscious indoctrination, Jorgen has fallen in with a crowd of smooth-talkers. The Back to Life movement is all cults everywhere fashioned after an afternoon in the Tyrol with many Nazi white beasts wearing lederhosen, chewing rock-dry plums and pears, angrily. Mia falls in with them too, as you do when your lover is a pin-up of Germany with perfect teeth smiling and you want to follow him to the ends of wherever he is going.

THIS IS THE BARN SCENE. This is the singing in the barn scene. These are the raised arms and blissed-out faces. This is the way. Follow the way. Come into the light. Come into the tunnel. Come here, to the honey-nectar. Come here to the third eye blinded by a world gone mad. The wolves scatter through these streets in their stolen clothes. They are ready for a change. They are ready to become dogs, to slip their heads into collars, to hang out around the food bowl, to scuffle about excitedly on the linoleum when we get home.

Here are the singers. White women, white willows. Here are the white men. Their eyes are on fire, in red. Here is the leather-bound Chamber of Commerce. Here are the gavel and the wig. Here are the swishing skirts of the dancing virgins. Here is the intentional clearing hankering after the shade. Here is the barn built on unceded territory.

Through a gap between the two barn doors Hilda and Dr. Grebing can see most of what is going on. A priest figure stands in front of a crowd of swaying singers. Mouths sleepy with joy spill the heavy notes of a hymn across the hay-specked floor.

"He looks really into it," says the doctor. "Is that Mia beside him?"

"Yes, she's part of this too."

"Really? Mia? Our teenage rebel with the gangbanged hair?"

"She had to find something to do. They look good together. Look. They're swaying in exactly the same way and in time with the music."

"Nice."

They watch for a long while, trying to think of what to do next. Then Hilda notices something moving at the back of the room.

"What's that?"

The doctor turns his head to the left and jams his eye up into the gap between the two heavy doors.

"Looks like figures. Black and whites. Etched types."

Hilda and Dr. Grebing hurry around the back of the barn and find knot holes in the wood to peer through. They see the entire cast of *Vedute di Roma* hanging around at the back of the barn, leaning on crutches and sticks, bent over their hungry bellies trying to clutch in some sustenance with their fingers, practicing the arm-outstretched spare-a-penny look.

"What are they going to do with them? Where did they come from?" asks Hilda.

"They're from all over the world. Take any city. Imagine its homeless, destitute, and criminal class and you've got yourself a Piranesi figure on your hands. I have no idea what they're going to do with them."

As if on cue, the crowd up front stops singing and moves to either side of the barn so that the priest can directly address the figures at the back.

"Come here, my people!" he bellows from his beard encircled residential school anus of a mouth.

The figures start to move towards the front, slowly, limping, helping one another along. There are children here too, and they come forward shyly, hiding in the nests of their mothers' skirt-legs.

"We are here to help you. If you would like to join us, we offer you the chance to have eternal happiness, good vegetarian food, free love, and a roof over your heads. In exchange, you need to wipe those pitiful looks off your faces and go out and get jobs like the rest of us."

Hilda watches Jorgen at this last comment, her socialist lovebird. She can see he is unsure about what the priest has just said, but on top of that uncertainty is pasted a gooey smile. Hilda can see he is too far gone.

A new song starts, erupts spontaneously from the mouth of a particularly zealous young convert. The figures hum along nervously, trapped in the centre of a sea of blissful, swaying blondes. Some of the figures fall down in exhaustion and are immediately lifted by strong, happy men and women that confuse the figures' collapsed bodies with their saved souls.

AFTER THE CEREMONY IS OVER, Jorgen finds Hilda and Dr. Grebing sitting by a tree outside the barn. They are cross-legged and deep in meditation. He nudges Hilda with his foot and she opens her eyes.

"What are you doing here?"

"We came to get you out."

Mia walks up and puts her arm through Jorgen's.

"Oh, we've come to this, have we? Public displays of affection?"

"Mia, can you give us a minute?" Mia shrugs and walks off towards the barn.

Jorgen crouches down and strokes Hilda's cheek with his feather-tipped fingers.

"You can't have me," says Jorgen. "Just like you couldn't have your father. Just like you haven't been able to have any of the men in your life—even your unborn son. God has me now."

Hilda spits on the ground.

"Is this what you call being yourself? Didn't you hear what Bill said at the beginning? You can be anyone? Why would you choose to lose your identity and be swept along on this carpet ride with a bunch of racists?"

"Racists?"

"You're all white. Except for the etched ones, and it's only their outlines that are black."

"Does that make us racist?"

"Of course. Don't you know that Hitler is coming? That he's almost here?"

Jorgen looks ashamed.

"Too busy sneaking around to notice what's going on in *History Book*. And it's right there in front of you."

Jorgen looks to where Hilda is pointing. *History Book* is there on the grass, open, smug. He can see that famous moustache fluttering back and forth in the wind of perfect timing.

THESE GENOCIDES BORN FROM THE AGGREGATE that makes the cult stand up. Stealing past the sleeping nun in her swastika print summer dress, the Secwepemc girl hoists her little brother up and over the school wall, scrambling after him along a moonlit trail back to grandmother. That night they are caught and returned. The belt is unleashed on the little bodies of those that would stand in the way of the whirr of progress, tip on the table, wet napkin, circle of the cocktail of pleasure and the spittle of the gold tooth shining like the body of a new Ford. In the morning their blood-striped backs push and push against the unflinching headlines of a Canadian newspaper.

"WELL, WHAT DO I DO NOW? I'm already in. I even have a title."

"What?"

"Head Recruiter."

"Some job you're doing. You've done nothing but turn me off since the moment you joined this clan of clowns."

Hilda stands up and puts her hand out to Jorgen. He pauses like in the movies and then, letting his relief slip out in the form of a great sigh, takes her hand in his.

"Coming?" Hilda calls to the others.

"Is it really this easy?" asks Mia, walking back over. "To leave? I thought there'd be a fight. Me pulling Jorgen one way, you pulling him the other way, my post-anorexia arms losing miserably."

"I've got an idea!" says Jorgen. "Let's have the priest chase us!"

Suddenly the four of them are off, rushing like mice from an illuminated kitchen. The priest and his minions are immediately after them, waving pitchforks. Goodbye. The river is icy on their ankles. Goodbye. The train is waiting for them on the tracks. Goodbye. Their arms wave from the train windows.

"Where now?" asks Mia.

"We have some work to do, right Hans? You guys can go back to sneaking around behind my back if you like."

"Sure," says Jorgen.

AWAY FROM THE WORDS IN THE STORY spills the news. Fascism. World Affairs. Current Events. Six cheeses in a pie. They die. They die.

Tale of the Small Green Weeds

IX

THE SWARMING PERSECUTED note the spit of religion's blasphemy. The bile of disappointment is strung in the trees for all to see. All manner of hatred buzzes angrily at its fruit. All smite. All smitten.

The blood of infidelity showers down on the hills and forests, pours into the lake so that it overfloweth. The sneaking rut of sodomy steals boys from their mothers' teats and chars Hell against their secret legs. All singing is glorified and exalted, raising the church roof with the collective breath of children and their pederast caretakers. The tribe's babes pretend to listen to the sales pitch of salvation, all for a smidgen of education, a chance out, by marriage, by plane, by sign on the dotted line, lead on by the hand of some white stranger with mothball breath.

The cult that nobody calls a cult beckons all wagons in and leads horses to suck at its trough of holy water, even though they'd rather not. Gaiety is in among the cedar and spruce. Women's bellies rise, dough in airing cupboards, full of holy fetal matter, because the vision is to spread the word out, like a permanent ink stain, like cancer. They meet in closed rooms, plot salvation on the heathen masses, throw crosses like darts at the reserve.

THE ATHEIST DELICATELY LICKS AT HER FINGERS. She loves the metallic taste of capitalism. She sprawls in the hot tub with her sexuality throbbing, ripping the stones out of plums with her mouth teeth lips. Her capture is inevitable. She will circle back on Sunday school when she is all grown up and has children of her own and she will tear down the roof with her bellowing praise of our Lord Jesus Christ, amen!

THERE IS NO KEEPING THE MISSION AT BAY. It parks its praise-be-the-lord bus and spews its chit-chatty, earnest-eyed youth out onto the grass. A child in donated shorts picks up his football and hides it behind his back. They can take his soul, but they can't take his football.

Forty

Dr. Hans Grebing has crossed lines with his laughing eyes, lines that wrap around Hilda as threads and draw her in a dancer. His wife is hardly part of this novel, but it is worth mentioning that she's never believed in his singing voice and that she spends too much time with her animals—a whole zoo of them, replacements for the children she has but doesn't like.

Hilda's breasts are glorious on film. Inescapable. Her teeth are bold white ornaments rooted in healthy bone. There are weaknesses in her body, as there are in all bodies, but we don't remember their names.

Although Hilda's tummy hangs wrinkling when she is on top, she is the heroine here. Hans longs for her hand that he brushed with his own in the parking lot; he longs to break the stillness of the afternoon with her confession of love poured over his.

Their office is too big for an affair. Nobody can corner or be cornered. There are so many excuses to slip out from under him. A lamp turned on at the main desk on a winter's evening takes me away from this July heat wave. They are moths for the art and each other. They grace the centre. He and she. Oh, release them from the pain of waiting. His fingers must slide into the emancipation of betrayal. His tongue must speak her name. A quiet curse against a mirror. And his wife must see it all for what it is and come hunting Hilda with her riding whip.

HILDA HAS THE PILE OF ART WORK that makes this scene a scene and does little else. She is moving through it slowly, twisted piece by twisted piece, turning it to get the angle right side up. Are these the legs? Is this the head? She gives the doctor time to read the images too. Their bodies are so close that we can smell their breath; snow pads against the window, muffling their determination.

"We're exploiting these people," Hilda says, turning to look the doctor in the eye.

"I know."

She looks sad from head on, but from the side, the view that Hans has, she looks like a forty-year-old who knows how to fuck in red hair and sweat. Nobody can free the field trip of artists now. Their bodies are body parts; their bones are who knows where. Microcosmic dust. Heavenly motion. Blood under the bridge.

Who burned us, who? Who burned us up? Who burned us, who? Who burned us?

We burned in the belly, in the beast. We burned in the chamber. Us ladies of great pleasure. Us men of great gloominess. We burned in the room, breathing smoke, breathing fire.

"Their art is all that people will remember."

HILDA PUSHES THE ART ASIDE and hops up onto the desk. Opening her legs, underwear conveniently removed when she went to the bathroom and the plan began, and splaying her vulva with her fingers, she says to the doctor, "What do you see?"

At first he cannot tell what it is, but soon he clearly sees a frog's head and body emerging from her vagina. One leg is stuck for a moment, still inside. The frog splays out its hands on the desk and pulls until the leg emerges, fully extended, bringing her juices with it.

"A frog."

"What else?"

He looks again. Now he sees the head of a mouse, no, a rat emerge. It looks from side to side, sees only her thighs, pulls its whole body out, letting the tail emerge slowly and with a mind of its own.

"A rat."

"What else?"

Over the course of the evening he sees a great many animals come out of Hilda's body, one after the other, none bigger than a squirrel, none smaller than a snail. They move away from the humans, exploring the large office, finding places to hide, finding water sources, crumbs.

Once the creatures cease—they wait, but nothing emerges—Hilda and the doctor know that she has become the painting of a woman suffering. Emma Hauck's word columns scrawling animal tracks out of the centre of her feminine wiles, being found worthy of some darker source. The kiss of the one who takes. The quiet surrender of the one who is taken. They are moving for each other. He presses up against her with his beloved erection. She, spent by all manner of fauna, wet from the delight of their trafficking paws and tails, yields to the surprise of his sudden body.

And it is love, my pet, my snake, my dangerous exotic creature. The office light hums against the flurries of night-winter; the room is full of stillness and delight. It is the room of painters, quiet now, bereft of creativity. His soprano. Her watercolours. The knitting needles of determined, infertile dreamers clacking over the booties of despair. He sings into her, his rain of tiny ladies and gentlemen. And one of them becomes a baby that is born in the sequel to this novel.

Forty-One

THE ASYLUM HAS BEEN DONE. We won't do it here. All we'll get is rocking back and forth; the odd scene of restraint; god in simplicity. They fill the swimming pool with their noise. Children trapped in the bodies of men and women, flailing gloriously, buoyed by the chlorinated soup.

The doctor knows that he is a kind man, building bridges, eliminating prejudice. The figures' art sits before us on the table. We make it what it is and what it is is beautiful. Suddenly our differences seem trivial.

On the quiet sofa Hilda sits waiting for Piranesi to show. Her hands are meat retaining water. She wishes she had removed her rings before the heat wave hit. The snow has been packaged up and put into storage. The sound of leafing through is all that can be heard.

Piranesi has been angry for months, mad at the Italian public—so hell bent on rush hour—mad at progress, mad at the garbage everywhere. History is sacredly being desecrated from all angles; even the pants of the beggars are falling down. Give them little ropes! Give them belts, even.

He's come to Germany for some fresh ideas. Mia sent for him because she wanted someone to distract Hilda from the dastardly cleavage of her Girls Gone Wild body pressed up against Jorgen. Piranesi stands in the doorway waiting for Hilda to notice him.

Come in, she says with her hand when she finally looks up. She recognizes him from the covers of many magazines. He's as you would expect. Salvador Dali with all the trimmings missing; the stereotypes of southern Europe bristling through his dark eyebrows, tingling along the bridge of his nose. He's carrying the blueprints for a new city.

"Look at these people!" he cries, coming into the room and stabbing his finger at his most recent etching. "They need someone to notice them!"

Hilda takes the sheet of paper from him and spreads it out on the coffee table. She recognizes three of them from Mia's stories, strokes their black-outlined skin, tidies their unbrushed hair with her pinkie nail.

"But can they make art?"

"Of course they can. Who can't?"

"Some people."

"I've yet to meet a person who can't make art. Cross a twig over another twig, put a leaf to the side of the cross, and you have a composition, a flag of sorts, an emblem. We can all do that."

He sits down beside Hilda and tickles her neck with his fingers, scrabbling round the back, under her red waterfall of hair, round the front, over her necklaces—too many for one neck—and down the mouth of her blouse, just briefly. She shivers out a draft of pleasure. It is blesséd, with an accent.

Piranesi has become Hilda's best friend over the course of this scene. It's those fingers that have etched out a reasonable excuse to love. Those fingers that have made us look at the tyranny of prison, the sorrow of abandoned buildings skirted by drunks, beggars and prostitutes. He houses them all. Little darlings, waving their walking sticks at Wordsworth and his band of hippies, saying, "There ain't nothing sublime about methamphetamine!" They emerge from the lead dust coughing blood out onto Hilda's palm. She sees why Mia is so fragile. This lot are her people.

She puts them down on the desk, the same desk that she and the doctor made love on, and gives them stamp-sized pieces of paper and little threads of wood dipped in black ink to draw with. They set to work immediately because they want to be part of the Grebing Collection after the war has swept away all the dark-hearted, migraine-plagued sociopaths that tried to put a stop to that rolling-down-hill-and-collecting-debris-on-the-way kind of artistic expression. Mad and sexual and terrifying. The large head of eyes peering into the ant-infested bowels of trauma and picking, one by one, the tiny rocks that have lodged there and carrying them off into infinity, on six thin legs.

Our insect men and women are sketching away happily, oblivious to their fate as words.

"Are you going to collect Mia while you're here?"

"My muse? She might help . . . No. I'm here to see you, Hilda. News of your Aslan-like presence has spread all over the wood. I am here to bow down at your feet. Quiet-wombed jewel of the Rhine, gentle mother of all that groan and rock, sweet caretaker of a husband who is faithful on one page, unfaithful on the next . . . " She puts her hand over his mouth to silence him.

"Do you know how angry I am?"

"No angrier than anyone else."

"Oh, yes. More. I rage at the heat. I rage at the crack. I rage at the empty packet. I rage at the dog's paws. I rage at the wet towel. I rage at the wind in my hair, flicking in my eyes and mouth, tormenting me. I rage at the words of my man and the women that he impregnates. I rage at my unborn babies. I rage at the quietness of afternoons. The burn. The cut. The broken stool. The dropped bag of rice. I rage at the river for not stopping for me. I rage at my feet in the cold water for being so old."

"Here. Come. I will run the artist in my fingers all over your skin."

"It won't do any good. Every scene in this book ends with a tender moment between a man and a woman, but the reality is things aren't getting any better."

"What do you have to complain about?" Hilda looks over at the desk and sees that one of Piranesi's figures has put down his thread of wood and is looking right at her. The others, watching this, begin to put down their tools and to gather around him. They are all looking over at Hilda, waiting for her to answer the question.

"I've got my problems; you've got yours. It's all relative," Hilda responds.

"Well, I wouldn't quite put it that way," says Piranesi, butting in. "These figures really do have quite a rough time. Basic needs aren't met. Their meals are never placed predictably in front of them. Each day, they embark on a brand new mission to find whatever it is their bodies and their children's bodies are in need of. Each day consists of a series of disappointments with the odd lucky break thrown in. And throughout this there is physical pain and mental anguish beyond any that we can imagine."

"We don't need you to speak for us, thank you," says one of the figures, a woman. "We can speak for ourselves."

"I'm sorry," says Piranesi. "I've just gotten so used to your silence over the years. You've always just been there, in the streets. You've been very good to me, you know—providing me with scale for my buildings, with a metaphor for the ruins of Rome."

"That's just the problem," says the figure that spoke first. "We're not like buildings. We don't represent the past. Not even slightly. We represent the present. We're here now. We're in every city. We are Everyman."

"And woman," pipes in another of the figures.

Herein lies the problem of this book, of my life, of yours. A marriage can fall apart, a sheet can slip from a lying wife or husband, a baby can hang out in the stratosphere skimming stones at your crying head for eternity, but nothing will ever compare to going hungry in a mean, wet-cold-in-the-bones street.

Piranesi and Hilda walk over to the table and open their hands out for the figures to climb on. Together they walk back to the sofa and lie down, side by side, being careful to hold the figures up and out of harm's way. Then they place them on their chests, where it is warm and soft.

For hours Piranesi and Hilda lay side-by-side, eyes closed, eyes filled with tears, listening to the mice in these people go about their daily survival of the fittest. As the hours pass, the tiny figures begin to talk, to get to know each other, to pool together their collective resources and allot each other roles and responsibilities. By nightfall, they have formed a collective and are ready to protect and defend one another at any cost. They are not the lone wolves of the *Vedute di Roma* anymore. They are a tribe. They are the stars of the Tale of the Small Green Weeds, brushing up on their acting skills, memorizing their lines, ready to tell their stories.

AT THE END OF THE DAY HILDA IS QUIET, introspective. Piranesi knows that she is feeling guilty for her crybaby antics, for her tendency to throw Drama at every scenario like it is a lifesaver. It isn't. It never will be, despite her wish to wallow her way out of the darkness, to wail her way into salvation and inner peace.

"Hilda, it is easier to be alive if you can put your life into perspective, if you can remember that you are not the only one suffering," Piranesi says, squeezing her hand.

She looks at him, but she says nothing. She knows that as soon as the weather changes she'll be right out there, running over the Moors with her rage sparking from the ends of her hair.

Tale of the Small Green Weeds

X

ROME IS A CITY WORN DOWN by the straps of camera bags. He put me against the column and shot me. I was at my sexual peak, part of the cast of *Thirtysomething*. There was always some man's hairy arm reaching over my dinner plate to adjust my clothing. The glitter of lust in his eyes.

I trace the inscription on the arc with my Braille finger and feel the shudder of plunder and rape. This will do nicely. And pocketing the guide book I draw my finger along the colour-coded streets in search of his pyramid. Caius Cestius was a philanthropist by default, found himself in the mood for giving, gave liberty as if it were his to give and then went into his tomb and turned off the light. The grave robbers came meticulously. The grave robbers kept their fingernails clean. They left nothing but the skeleton blueprint of Vegas, which sat like a cicada in the cold tomb waiting to burst upon the imagination of an architect like a Catherine wheel.

Ah! The tragedy of the life span.

Forty-Two

VIOLET IS STILL BLEEDING, but only slightly. She's moved beyond the raw rub of sorrow into the quiet hum of relief. She didn't want Stephen's baby anyway. She finds the Non-Catholic Cemetery because she is temporarily spiritual and in need of a quiet meditative moment over a grave or two. Keats and Shelley will do.

Keats was just an expat asking for *cafè amb llet*. He probably had a receding hairline or pale, flabby buttocks. But there was so much Dean Moriarty obsession back then that the girls just did whatever the guys said, even after a stillbirth when the afterbirth was stuck and infected and she throbbed at the grave like a drum. There was no support group or literature to read in the waiting room or manners at the bedside. It was just another dead baby.

Violet sits on the grass and wonders at the space writ on water. These two clever ruffians and their lovehearts share a space with the wealthy and thick. In death, poets become millionaires texting stanzas from the back seats of limousines. They are on the road, finding ancient things in ancient places, texting Google maps. Come down to the river, boy lover. Come to the party and watch me fuck her.

VIOLET WILL NEVER BE A WRITER. She is dead now. She's been dead for over forty years. On her hospital grave-bed she caught the chubby one-year-old girl-me and kissed my neck. She doesn't even get to paint in this book, not even with the offhanded slash of Japanese rice in a field. Not even black on white. Not even a doodle on a telephone book.

She is just a quiet mother reeling from her own stupid mistakes, putting her head on gas mark high for 40 minutes, while the children scream and scramble over her hips.

There is always a chair in this memory that isn't mine. She kneels and rests her head on the chair, wig removed and placed on the floor, as if for the guillotine. She is a queen stripped of her paraphernalia, which once made her separate, distinct from her people, which made her mother, the woman who owns the leg that I am tugging on. And then it's all Sylvia Plath on us and Gwyneth Paltrow shoving the loving cloths of "I'm sorry" between the door frame and the floor. But not that. Not that at all. Because this is merely a threat, shouted at Tom Sawyer, who runs sobbing outside right into a game of beat up the kid who wets his trousers. Only that isn't happening because it happened too long along and too faintly to trace. Violet thought she had no reason to live. She hugged little Madame Bovary and little Tom Sawyer that one time, but that was all. And then the women in this book were shaken out of the blanket and went rolling across the floor into the paths of the men. And that was just one shake, just one method of building a narrative.

Forty-Three

JORGEN IS AFRAID TO TAKE ACTION. He is all thought, trapped in the heavy morass of "what if?" The woman beside him is fading, wearing thin. The great fear in her, poor lamb, is that he will abandon her, leave her for someone young and fresh and free of charge, who throws herself at him across a launderette in a beautiful arc.

This isn't the fairy tale his mother adlibbed over his little-boy head. Hilda has grown plain to him, even if to us she is on fire, and there is nothing that turns him off more than her crying face when she is yet again not pregnant at the beginning of a new chapter.

Who is this man? German. Jorgen. Artist (for joy) turned carpenter (for money). Weak at the knees for a good rhetorician. Startled at midlife by the body that is still his, dripping with water as he hoists himself up out of the blue pool of homosexuality, heavy with muscle grown in the roots of my orgasm. Blue-eyed and blond because it matters to someone. A Scorpio, for the secrets. Raised by a widow. Some siblings here and there. A father who comes via a photograph and gets replaced by the leader of a cult that puts healthy thighs and big, strong arms on his list of Things to Do.

He is so perfect to Hilda—our dripping with pool-water

demi-god—that she ogles him from the window when he walks up the path to the house. We know how Hilda feels because she is a female character, a part of me, but we cannot access Jorgen without a knife.

It is not easy to look inside a man. There may be something simple there—something regular and plain and normal, a lack of complexity, no motive to harm or abandon or possess at the throat for a joke, just a joke, but it isn't funny when it's your own throat. And the hands of this man are spanning out like hawk wings, beating swiftly in the hot night air, a loud conundrum. Do we trust him, this bird of prey? This tall man of reason? This Aryan pin-up?

He is at the root of German-me, the halls at Heidelberg full of my family. Somehow we were watered down into this fine mess of mental health, hardly a thing to worry about, but you do, you know? You just do. Because where else did he come from, this man that I need to take care of and worry about? He is some kind of father, brother, cousin. He is to be trusted—even with Mia at the mouth of his river—because he is an innocent liar, a sweet drunk at the work party sucking some married woman's tit.

Follow him. I do. See where he goes. I do. I am never horrified or shocked or even bothered, really. He's every stereotype the TV has to offer. I am weak to have created him this way. A cheat. A quiet one at that. Speaking up only after he has been led astray by the Back to Life movement and become some sort of spokesperson for the cause. He drains the earwax out of Hilda's listening skills day in day out, until eventually she asks him to leave. He does. With Mia. His confidante and sidekick. Hilda is not afraid. She cannot love a man, anyway. She can only observe him warily, waiting for him to abandon her and her unborn children.

Poor Jorgen is none of these things. Jesus was a carpenter.

Poor Jorgen has been led to believe. Has been taken on reluctantly by the part of me that knows what's good for me. Forgiveness, my gentle act, my one-act play staged quietly on the pages of *More House*, was mainly for therapists that might be looking. The dark circle of wonder still spins heavily around me, my women, my cast. How can Jorgen be somebody I can trust?

I give him a Jesus job. I give him quiet, honest eyes. I make him handsome. I give him jobs to do, seasons to work through, a playlist of great songs, a socialist heart. He betrays me only because I make him.

HILDA SOBS ON JORGEN'S CHEST IN THE DARK ROOM. There is nobody else here to listen to her crying, to comfort her. He's tired, weary of her emotional outpourings. This is woman. This is man. What silly markers of nothingness! Jorgen soaks his hairy body in the bathtub, lost in the landscape of the ceiling with its various webs and spiders, cracks and marks, its quiet presence in the face of all of us. We are so special. We are so real.

Jorgen flips over the record on the gramophone. Future Islands. Growling. The sea is rising somewhere out there in the future. Islands are coming out of the mainland, finding closure and solitude. Jorgen takes one island. Hilda takes another. Mars. Venus.

Give me more time to prove myself. I will find his heart in my hands throbbing to the beat of my own. It will look like meat, like mine; it will feel like blood, which is different from water, and the blood will be Hilda's pinkish-brown shout, day 29, day 30, his arm around her because he is not the one bleeding. Just wishing he was.

Forty-Four

JORGEN HAS BEEN SALT AND PEPPERED FOR GQ. He enters Hilda's vision in the high street in his flagrantly beautiful, defying all reason body. Stopped in her tracks by his violent magnetism, she watches him walk. Her teenage body re-emerges deep inside her, which she knows will dissipate quickly, leaving her just the high street and the husband.

Today they are meeting with someone to discuss adoption. He needs the wind to change direction, to expend the waft and weave of middle-aged poetics on something with two arms, two legs, and a head. He doesn't know if anything will come out of this meeting. He just knows that he needs his wife to find a new obsession.

"Are you sure you want to do this?" she asks, walking a little ahead of him and talking back to him as if he were her dawdling child.

"We're just going to talk to her. That's all."

"What's her name again?"

"I can't remember. Does it matter?"

"Well, it shows we're serious, that we've done our homework, that we remember names and figures and dates and things."

"Figures and dates of what?"

"I don't know. My last period. How long we've been trying. Whether we've consulted a doctor about it. How many times a week we . . . "

"Hilda! Stop. Just stop." He takes her hand, pulls her back and in line with him. "Just stop, OK. Breathe."

She listens because he is wise man of the woods all of a sudden and because a deep breath does one a world of good, like a cup of tea, like a good cry, like a swim in cool water with seaweed way down deep waving alive alive oh on a shimmy of fish. For that, you may need goggles or, even better, a mask.

Her deep breaths are more like sighs. She's going to lose this magazine man if she doesn't stop her depression. It barrels on, disregarding all warnings, crashing down into the ravine of middle age, wearing leopard print and waxing its prickly bikini line. He will not stick around much longer to listen to her cry.

"OK. I'm OK."

She squeezes his hand to let him know things that we cannot know because they are between a wife and a husband. And even though the sex has skulked up into their aging centres, it has not gone away completely, not even close. Here, there is a quiver. There, there is an urge. So vile. So sweet. Recoil outright the reproductive space that is so quiet we do not notice it until it is too late.

Pulled under, again, Hilda. Come back to us. Come and feel the stone underneath your feet. So many of us have walked over it, bent double in pain, floating in love, held up like puppets by our children with the dementia coming up behind like a gust of wind. On the wing, Hilda, get on the wing and then settle down your pattering feet here, in this seaside town that is still open at all hours and has donkeys and tea, of course, and cream-filled rip offs of French pastries. The clouds roll on in thunderous apocalypse but your hand is in his and that hand it slays us to our early graves in love and fingers us back alive, below there, such tenderness, such warmth, blow there, blow at the heat of summer that pools in the crevices of your marriage, shake out the weather in sheets of sweet agony.

He is your gift, there beside you on the street, in the car, at the table, in the bed. Yours to have for free! The body of a man inside your house, hard for you, grasping for your happy body.

Hilda stops walking, Dr. Grebing's ladies and gentlemen jiggling somewhere inside her. She knows that she will birth The Miserables. She will mother the wretches, the vagabonds. They will scatter out in their adorable onesies into Piranesi's *Vedute di Roma*. Some limping. Some leaning.

"I don't want to do this. I've changed my mind."

Jorgen sighs.

"Why?" he says.

"I don't know. I just have a feeling that I shouldn't ever be anyone's mother. I won't be a good mother. I'm cruel. I shout too much. Violet and I are like sisters, learning bad habits from each other. Florence is the only nightingale at the nursery window building lullabies out of the air. Florence has a gentleness that I didn't inherit. My hair is a rage of sorts. My uniform is tight around my Kate Winsletness. I am selfish at the best of times, morbidly self-obsessed at the worst. I cry into pillow cases because handkerchiefs, that awful word, aren't big enough."

Hilda wants to be an artist. An artist is a mother of the page. Her children are made of paper. They are paper dolls repeating a certain style that cannot escape from the pages of *More House*. Artists aren't able to fix the child's broken dreams — there are so many. The child comes crying out of the swimming pool because the threat of drowning overwhelms her. And the artist writes about it. Secretly luring over the choking child's face to catch the authenticity of the moment.

"I will not put on an act for the woman at the adoption office."

Hilda is clear headed and she looks pretty. Jorgen treats her to tea and a scone. This is the Margate high street of Germany. I see from the airplane that the surrounding fields are green as green can be. The Rhine snaking through the Narnian hills and valleys promising towns and strongholds.

Forty-Five

SOMEHOW THEY REACH THE BUILDING where the adoption agency is housed. It's on the second floor and the window overlooks the parking lot where my cold nipples protruded through my T-shirt after swimming in the sea. This is no Thai paradise. This is Margate, again.

Hilda goes straight to the window and looks out while Jorgen engages in small talk. She's the same woman that interviewed Hilda earlier in the novel and then told her she'd make a good nurse. She's got the same bright, vacant smile on her face, as if there's nothing in her but the light of Jesus.

"Please sit down, Mrs. German Surname. Here, Mr. What's Your Pickle, take my seat."

Perching on the desk, with her legs too close to Hilda's man's legs, she starts to ask questions. Small, pretty ones at first—like, "Have you come here from work?" or "Nice outside?" (There's the window, thinks Hilda. See for yourself)—and then leading to more complicated beasts like "How long have you been considering adoption?"

Damn this fucking woman, thinks Hilda. How dare she be the gatekeeper of motherhood!

The questions persist. The woman starts to look at her file of papers, to make tick marks here and there, to take brief notes, missing important details so that Hilda and Jorgen must slow down, repeat things.

After half an hour of this, she puts down her pen, shuffles her papers together and gives another of her bright, lit from the inside Christian smiles. No teeth, all condescension.

"Well." She pauses. "I think we can move on to stage two of the process at this point."

"Which is?" asks Hilda in a kind of bitchy tone that she didn't feel coming until it was too late.

"Meet the kids!"

At this, she rises from the desk, papers in one hand tucked against her body as if shields were instinctual, pen in the other. Then she swings the door wide open. "Ta da!"

In the hallway, crowding in to get a look at their new mommy and daddy, are children with shaved heads and striped pajamas, fresh from a Nazi concentration camp. Suddenly, out of their silent confusion a cacophony of pleas erupts, spoken, shouted, in more than one language, rising, rising to compete with each other, "Please take me out of here!" "I beg you to save me!" "Don't leave me here to die!"

The woman shuts the door, pushes her body against it, smiles a romantic-comedy smile and pushes her glasses up the bridge of her nose. And even though she is sexy underneath them, a footballer's wife for sure, she must wear glasses so that the audience will be tricked into thinking she is intelligent as well as sassy, funny, klutzy, and even a little goofy. She's perfect for the role.

"Wrong door," she laughs. "It's this one."

She reopens the same door with another "Ta da!" and there in the doorway stands a small girl, two, maybe three years old, in a blue and white sailor suit dress and ridiculously cute white fluffy cardigan that has the aura of detergent commercials about it, and in her hand is the rope of a red wagon and in the wagon is a forlorn-looking bunny, sagging over slightly but not too much or the set director will be pissed, and she says, "Mommy? Daddy?"

She is perfect. Untouched. Nobody has hurt her or hurt anyone around her. A dog has never been kicked in her presence. Snails have not been crushed, rushing from the car to the house after rain. Even flower heads have not been plucked. No bird has crashed into the window of this child's life and then fallen, feet pronged upwards, head slightly turned as if it were the neck that snapped (it was), with a small drop of some kind of bird plasma on the concrete beneath its tiny corpse. Nobody has raised their voice or gotten stressed out or almost drowned her in the bathtub by accident. Nobody has forgotten for a moment that she was in the back of the car. There have been no accidents and no on-purposes. Hitler has kept her in a glass case that he winds up in the morning so he can watch her twirl during breakfast. She is all the perfect children of northern Europe that taunt us with their free daycare and genderless toys. Wisps do fall from her braided hair, but never too many and never too few. Her cheeks are warmed in the streusel-y kitchen, where she cuddles with a grandmother with sweet breath.

"Where did those other children go?" asks Hilda.

"Oh, back to Nazi Germany. They have History to contend with. Never a pretty thing."

"But I want one of those. There was a boy there. He had dark eyes. He didn't say much. He might have turned into a drug addict or a recluse or an I don't know what, but I'm trained. I can handle anything. I want that boy. Bring him back."

"I'm sorry, Mrs. German Surname, but he doesn't fit your

profile. You and Jorgen are looking for an unscarred child. See. It says so right here."

She holds the paper out for Hilda and points at the line that says, "We're looking for a child that is, you know, how do you say this? Jorgen? Help me, love . . . Umm . . . *Unscarred?*"

"I know I said that, but I've changed my mind. Doesn't intuition count for anything? I love him. He's my baby. I want him. Open that door. Open it. Now! Jorgen, tell her! Open the door. I want to save him. I want to save him from History. He belongs in Literature. In Fiction. With me. With Jorgen. We're a family. Please, please bring him to me!"

Hilda has slumped down onto the floor and is crying, sobbing in desperation, wanting to save her boy, knowing what will happen to him, knowing he is doomed, even if J.D. Salinger does show up pulling a crazy and graciously accepting bouquets of flowers, flowers that have found a way through the entire war in the rubble-free spaces away from buildings, where fields are still fields and hedgerows are still hedgerows. They will not liberate this particular boy. No. He will be good on that final day, but goodness won't count for much. Salinger will see his charred body but he will not adopt it or take it back to America on a ship. Hilda knows all this because she's seen the movie. She can't stand the helplessness and the feeling that she is complacent, a passive bystander watching the tanks roll by, knowing that peace is just a word at a spelling bee.

Jorgen has been silent all this time. He saw the children in their stripes. He saw the girl in her sailor suit. He observed them from the back of the room, felt pangs of fatherlove for each and every one of them.

"We shouldn't have come," he says. "Hilda said it was a bad idea, but then she came, we came anyway. Just to see. Just to ogle these children on the free airwaves that billow them as flags across the screen. We see them. Of course we do. We're here to look, to shop for a son or a daughter. But they know we're looking at them. They scream for us to take them away, to love them. We would if we knew how, but we don't. Hilda, we don't."

He reaches down and scoops her raggedy body up and off the office floor. The woman grimaces as she watches him lift his wife, a sheaf of material draped over his arms, and carry her through the doorway. The mirage of parenthood has lifted. There are no children to take home. The woman takes off her glasses, rubs the bridge of her nose, rubs her hands over her face to revive her skin and shake her out of this moment, this room. The scene has been a difficult one. She isn't used to surrealist French films descending on her like bats with faulty sonar. She's used to Romantic Comedies and Chick Lit. Without her glasses she is a babe. Without her glasses she looks vulnerable and perhaps a tad slow on the uptake.

She opens the door and the children come into the room. There are big bags of American-sized marshmallows in one of her desk drawers. The children have one each. They focus on the bubbles of air popping as the marshmallows dissolve in their mouths.

"OK. Back in, guys. They'll be another couple showing up any minute now."

Tale of the Small Green Weeds

XI

GAZA CHILDREN BOMBED THE SHOCK out of revolution waves still crashing Facebook it. The riot of the people I love. Text travels. Words get off the couch, leave the living room and have wing span and velocity. The articles patter in against the screen, one after the other, another dead child.

Revolution. Living room. Couch. TV.

The cars made it out of the city safely, were rerouted, occupants discussing the political strife going on down at the great square of community and cafés. These years of sweeping genocidal agendas have made atrocity a moot point. In *Autobiography of Red* Anne Carson says something about cars sleeping in their shadows. How apt. These little human Peter Pans, never taking responsibility for their crimes against humanity, so snug as a bug in a rug, we enter the city by tunnel, by night, the street lamps full of romance and promise. The car, so proud of its accomplishments that it gives off a little beep-beep of joy.

The city bows to the Moses-large handshake in the offices at Ford. A derelict city that attracts youth with SLR cameras, dark rooms made out of dark rooms, T-shirts functioning as camera bags. They document the truth that nobody wants to face: cars are not our friends; cars are not our salvation; cars do not maketh the man, however jaguar-esque or Greek myth-esque they pretend to be.

The car commercial creeps over the bombed-out city, sneaks between tuk-tuks, cuts off pedestrians. A flock of pigeons erupts. A body, dusty, streaked in blood, fresh kill, is hauled into the trunk and arranged according to its dimensions.

To view the video footage of atrocious human behaviour you must first watch the fifteen-second car commercial. How smooth and sleek! There she blows, deeper into the Pyrenees, past towns where hand-woven material flaps from windows and goats pass in all their poverty. The car stops, a sigh of envy interrupted by buildings that aren't buildings anymore, Sophoclean women in headscarves straining their crying faces for god to take into consideration. Great politician in the sky, they wail, see me, see my suffering and remove me from this car commercial.

And still the rivers of traffic pulsate greedily through the killing fields, through the suburban pharmaceutical experiment, through the ghettos that cling to the outskirts of the city, through the wide-open spaces and tunneling forests that are not cars, not freeways.

These cyber trails of information must exist once more at the expense of human interaction. How quickly the party folds itself up and goes away. How briefly the ticker tape celebration lasts, even in a photograph, compared to the years of turmoil, hatred, bloodshed, and hyper hyper eggshell anxiety, son in the city, with friends, out late, the curfew descending upon him, the shelling refusing to sleep.

The bomb is the gay invention of boys in childhood. Whizzing and fizzing like a Roald Dahl sentence, smoothly arched, gymnastic, it sends flowers of dust, spits snowballs of rubble at the kids' heads, their game cancelled by death, the cricket pavilion closed for the unforeseeable future because you cannot know whether you'll be at the X of panic and destruction or if you'll be at-home watching TV or setting the table for your mom when it happens.

The baby is shelled. She is shelled out of her mother's arms, through a closed window, out into a dusty courtyard. Little spit of hate. Torn and blood-stained piece of debris. Her mother is blown in the opposite direction, into a wall, her milk letting down for no one.

Forty-Six

FLORENCE, IN HER PRETTY-FACED PERFECTION, swings in the darkness of the school playground as Stephen peacocks the monkey bars, change falling from his pockets onto the hard ground of my childhood. Her stomach turns as she swings, meaning that she is not a child anymore. This bothers her. She is not interested in being reminded that her body forgets to squat down into the realm of marbles or span cartwheels across the dandelion-ridden field. Saturday. No children to smash into in their small covens of play. No one to see her long limbs wheeling.

She has poor posture and a semi-permanent streak of pain that rivers down her right leg. The last baby, perhaps? Her mother-body, that heaved and bore down on the blood-specked sheet, gives over everything to bring life into this world. No amount of kisses and cuddles is too many. Her three children hover around her, checking in, needing reassurance, desperately unsure of their identities, unable to answer the gentleman's question, sweetheart, with a number or a name. I am four. My name is a word of love in your language.

Florence is in love for the first time. They are three children into their marriage, but up until now she has not felt love for Stephen. Affection, yes. Tenderness, too. But nothing like this feeling she has right now that breaks her insides and spills them out onto the playground, that heaves up into the summer trees and makes the leaves shiver and shake over the pavilion. This man before her, stomach exposed, shirt covering his face, fingertips brushing the ground as he swings back and forth, the same man that until this point was for all intents and purposes the love of her life, has suddenly pricked her heart alive. It is nothing to do with the way he looks or what he is doing. It is just that she has realized, right here, right at this very moment, that she is going to lose him.

STEPHEN AND FLORENCE HAVE BEEN DRINKING. For tonight, she's given up her vigil at the door of the spare room, praying through the keyhole in whispered spurts, and has decided to join him. He passes her the bottle, grabs it back from her before she can take a second swig. She snatches it from him, swills the hot, sharp liquid, and then throws the bottle across the field. It bounces off into the dark, dribbles out onto the grass.

"Why'd you have to go and do that?"

"It was empty."

"No, it wasn't."

Her emotions have packed up into tight-folded love letters stuffed in the back of a drawer. She looks over to the road, watches a car slow down, the driver peer out to see if he can assess what kind of mischief they might be up to. Florence fingers the driver and he picks up speed.

"He saw you," says Stephen.

"No, he didn't. It's way too dark."

Stephen has gone to pick up the bottle. She feels so sorry for him.

He returns, licking his fingers, drinking back the last of the whiskey.

"Stephen?"

"Uh."

"Why are you sleeping with Violet?"

"What?"

"Why are you sleeping with Violet?"

"I heard you the first time. I'm not."

"I've read the book already, Stephen. You can't deny it."

"Who gave you the book?"

"That's not the point. Why are you sleeping with her?"

Stephen rubs his face, sits on the swing next to Florence, facing in the opposite direction, looking at the old brick school lording it over them.

"I'm not. That's just a story. A little story that someone told someone else and then they told someone else and before I could pinch it to stop it from gushing its dirty content all over the basement floor, it fell upon your pretty ear, my love, my bird."

"Are you going to tell Violet that it's not true? That it's just a 'little story'?"

"Maybe. Should I? Won't she be upset?"

"I'm not sure."

"I mean what does she have to live for now?" asks Stephen. "Bill's long gone and she has no hair. If her wig slipped off in the middle of it, just slipped right off and fell on the floor, she'd be there with her no-hair head just right there in the arms of some motel guy and he'd probably still finish anyway. He'd close his eyes and finish and then he'd make up some excuse to leave."

"Is that how the story ends?"

"I'm not sure. Poor Violet. She could have been any of us,

but she chose to be her. Why would she choose that? Why would she choose to be a woman when she could have been a man? Why would she choose to live in London in a block of flats? Or smoke herself to death? Or be poor? Why be poor when you can be rich? Why be a single mother when you can have a husband? Why lose all your hair when you could keep all your hair? I'll never understand her, Florence, and perhaps that is why I'm sleeping with her."

"Perhaps. You always fall for a good sob story. So do I. That's what we have in common. A good sob story will always have us crying like a pair of lonesome dogs. Is that what we are, Stephen?"

"Drunken, crying, lonesome dogs on a school playground at night? Sure."

VIOLET TAKES OFF HER WIG and hangs it on a hook in the bathroom. The door is locked. She checks again to be sure. Her head is the head of death. The grim reaper leers over her right ear, licks at her baldness, laughs a crude, rotten laugh that gurgles the phlegm of homelessness and booze.

She hears the city raging outside. Tonight all the cities in all the world in all history have come to her London, her Hackney. The sound will tear her from her thoughts, keep her from sleep for days, weeks, even for a lifetime. These people are angry. These people, like me, she thinks, have picked at the wound of poverty. The cup does not overfloweth. There is love. It is true. There is memory and all its tender flecks and rivets. It cannot be denied. But here, in this roaring, burning mess of bombs and batons and boots, the money cannot lay itself down fast enough. Bill after bill after bill. The bank teller cannot free us from this tyranny.

She takes a cotton wool ball soaked in some darling liquid chemical and removes her left eyebrow. Then her right. The brown stain of eyeliner looks like shit on toilet paper. The shit of my life, she thinks. I must stare it right in the face of the evening news.

FLORENCE PUSHES BACK AND BEGINS TO SWING. Stephen follows her. They swing harder, higher. O, throne of childhood, where the world that spans out around your eyes is larger and more glorious than your little house on so-and-so street, so that you dream of going all the way round, just once, without first slamming down onto the metal bar and cracking your head open.

O, children, swing high on those sweet chariots.

Forty-Seven

BILL IS PHOTOGRAPHED WALKING DOWN The Streets of London, looking off to one side, looking straight into the camera, talking on his yet-to-be-invented cell phone. Pigeons flap into the composition around him, shot at all the right places with their choreographed feet and wings. A lonely alley cat rubs up against a lamp post just to the left of his Sunday shoe.

London is a photograph to me. It is memory in matte, swinging from my father's hammock, at the tail end of the 1970s. I find a woman in the kitchen in a shimmery dress that hangs from her shoulders on chains made from tiny balls of silver cake decorations, one hand holding a cigarette, the other holding a glass of red wine.

The landscape of childhood is infiltrated by the tendrils of spider plants, green doodles in the living rooms of hipsters, spilling out all over the furniture, clawed by kittens that disappear before turning into cats. They are in London, these rooms, but there is nothing remembered around them, so that they are housed at the level of vignettes only. Little stories.

Bill walks through these streets looking for solace. He

passes the room I am in, way before I am born, looks up at the window even, as if he knows that one day his granddaughter will be given visitation rights to his life in the form of this novel. His tenderness must be here. The weird moment in the kitchen when he tried to kiss me must be here. The darkness of his war-rage that he suspends in the portraits of war planes must be here. As must the puttering softness of his unschooled mind and the sunken eyes of his fey grandmother, so innocuous in her Woolworth's picture frame, just a black-and-white Cockney witch, reading tea leaves, being tender inside Bill's memory, small as a child despite the magnitude of her gift.

She knew that her grandson would lose his children. She could see that far ahead. But she didn't see far enough to know that he would find them again, dragging their tragedies with them so that he couldn't see for all the crying.

I TOOK BILL TO THE CHALKY COAST on the eve of his first stroke thinking that the sea air would bring Violet back, make him speak her name to me. He was a soldier. He didn't let up that he was tired, that I was killing him with my enthusiasm. We took rests on benches and then one more thing and one more thing took us back in history through the quiet town of Sandwich that was the gardener of my ambition for words that are green, brightly coloured, clouds, water, water boatmen, the churchyard and its various brands of shade brandishing the songbird at the throat of god, the warmth of renovated houses, owned by architects and engineers that take the train to London every morning and doze on the commute home.

I tell him about The Sinking Mud. He applauds me for not falling in and dying. A rowboat passes us. Someone is shelling the hell out of us. We don't duck for cover because the war is over. We order a "lovely lunch" and when I pick things from his plate he says nothing even though he is depressed by my lack of manners. By the evening, walking back to the train station, I realize that I have probably killed my own grandfather. I put him on the train. He leans from the window. I tell him to sleep on his way back to The Streets of London. I don't know that he never sleeps in moving vehicles in case he has to jump out, which he has, many times, falling, a gift of a man, the grandson of a clairvoyant, knowing his fate will be unavoidable, falling into meadows, into waves, onto corpses, roofs.

By the time he reaches Waterloo Station he is so exhausted that he wonders how he will get back to his flat. Will Hilda be there waiting to grill him about his trip? Will she suspect that his days are numbered?

Balmy, graced with women in shawls going to the theatre, men at their arms, on duty, London was his house and home. It took him an hour to get back to his flat. He walked slowly, sat on benches along the way, closed his eyes and prayed for things that he would not be granted.

THAT LAST DAY TOGETHER the smell of the sea drifted over the golf course, the marshlands, made the Netherlands seem like a sister, brought the smell of faraway places into the ruins at Dungeness, suggested the presence of lugworm trails, sea cabbage, and barbed wire. War zones, these beaches packed with families of tourists. Making love situational. A brief bivouac of P.K. Page poetry tousling the hair of sons and daughters in their swimming costumes, parading, buffooning out of the sands in the circus that is childhood.

I showed him my heaven. It smelled of a flowering privet hedge. It had the tang of sea air.

THE WET SAND STRETCHES OUT FOREVER and when he gets there, to the toes of the sea, he must walk further still to find a wave to engulf him and carry his swimming body away.

Tale of the Small Green Weeds

XII

IN THE QUIETNESS OF THE ETCHED PLATE the figures start to shiver and shake, rattling off their death songs with quiet determination. Who built this city? Who made this tourist cake party? Who stepped out of the cave of the subway into this financial district on spidery legs? Who tried to eat the paycheque, to nibble at its corners, to buy enough plastic toys to keep all the children happy for eternity?

Their rags are rich with suggestion. They drop their sticks and hoes and crutches, don magic wands that spin and spin in the quiet light of morning, a city waking, still smoking, glass crunching under foot, moving back into the steady pulse of capital gain and capital loss. The layoffs fire along the chain of being, leaving children walking barefoot through the rioted streets to schools that only test them on the fullness of their stomachs.

How the revolution moves like an Olympic sprinter plucked from adversity. Her body ploughs through the rules and regulations, dissolves nine, dissolves five, turns our houses inside out, lets the creeping ivy wallpaper the place, allows for fire pits to be dug into lawns, kitchens to be turned into meeting rooms.

The figures enter by the back door, hooded, quiet. There is only so much they can take before death becomes option B. There is only so much of a gap that can grow before the connection between rich and poor snaps completely and the pearls lay unshucked.

Here is every mother's son on TV, bleeding from the side of his head. A rock held out to a journalism student to take and bag as evidence. The sound of smashed glass lets the wind whistle on through, a new song, a new house, with nothing boarded up, nothing for sale.

Forty-Eight

"WHAT DOES IT FEEL LIKE TO LOVE A WIFE? Your wife?"

"To love Hilda? What does it feel like?"

"Yes." Mia crosses her legs and settles in for Jorgen's answer.

"It feels lucky."

"Lucky how?"

"Lucky as in you can close the door and she's all yours. Not as a piece of property. Not like that. She wants to be yours. Nobody can interrupt. They wouldn't dare. They wouldn't dare tap her on the shoulder and say, 'May I have this dance?' No, they wouldn't dare. Not because I'd fight them—although I would—but because they are too afraid that she will turn them down."

"How do you know she will turn them down?"

"Because I just know."

Mia stands up from the sofa and walks over to Jorgen.

"Can I be her for a while? Just for one day."

Jorgen kisses Mia on the mouth like it is the first time. A dance hall springs up around them. The hall of kissing his liquor-breathed dancing, pulling her close then pushing her away. He passes her to Bill who is dancing past, one-two-three, one-two-three, with a mop. The smell of bleach tinges the air, presses against the tenderness of the moment. "Here," says Bill, passing the mop to Jorgen who leans it against the wall.

One-two-three, one-two-three. Mia feels silly. This is some old man's dance hall. There are ashtrays on every table. They all need emptying.

"Where would you like me to take you?" Bills asks, smiling down at Mia's downy face.

"To the 1980s. To a David Bowie song," she says, hitching up her pant legs to avoid the wash of water that is spreading over the dance floor, fresh from the English Channel, salty and cold.

Bill dances her to the other side of the room where she can climb onto a bench and watch the show. He splashes off to the bar to buy her a drink as Piranesi, wearing reflective shades and a leather jacket, homes in on her wide, hopeful embrace. They will marry after all. After all her wandering lust has sizzled out. He is a boy, her boy, of her clan. He is tanned, T-shirted, a keeper of backseat secrets beside the winter road.

When they kiss it is their first kiss outside *The Italian Saga*. He tastes of cigarettes and alcohol. She cannot get enough of the taste of his rebellion. This is the first kiss. Ever. This is the tongue. This is the sweaty hand. This is the breath of the top 40 reigning over the DJ booth. The heat of bodies rippling up their wet backs.

The song stops. In that deep moment of silence she feels Dr. Grebing's mouth at her ear, breathing out a secret, a promise. The music starts again and they shimmy their way through it as best they can in the thick water that drowns their Sunday shoes.

And now Stephen enters with his Adrian Brody cheekbones, done up to the nines as the crowd parts to find room for Mia's glorification. She sees a newt, a crisp packet, a fleet of bobbing plastic cups around her shins, but her feet move through the dance anyway, splashing Stephen's trousers.

"Dance with me, too," she says. And of course he does, ignoring the crowd of tourists fattening themselves on roasted pig, laughing and shouting in their thick groups, tightened closer by their accents, their pale, flaccid skin, their bulging alcohol wombs.

The tourists are thinning out, moving out of the dancehall and off down the beach, leaving Piranesi's figures to vacuum up the dirty water, throw out all the garbage bags, full and dripping with juice, to follow the parasites' trash trail down to the water's edge, where their beer cans and plastic water bottles will begin their quiet, lonely drift into islands.

All the men—Jorgen, Bill, Piranesi, Dr. Grebing, and Stephen—sit together on the sand watching Mia dance closer to the sea. They search their wallets for the cash to have her little Thai body, while they fight over who paid for the last meal, the last hookers. Once they stop arguing, they can just hear the troop of tourists far down the beach attempting to carry each other's falling laughing bodies into the waves.

They call to her, plead with her to come back to them, but Mia is nowhere to be seen. Figment. Filament. Gone back to *The Italian Saga* to rest in peace.

Tale of the Small Green Weeds

XIII

THE CLEAN VIDEO LINES of Golden Rome that whir from the Betamax deceive Art History into thinking that it was once a George Lucas space city.

It was always just a city, blushing perfectly here, rotting quietly there.

Rotting quietly there. Then loud. Then louder. Screaming, even. As the cut glass shopping spree spreads its filth through the photojournalist's dreaming morning story. This frenzy of stuff will not deliver us from the trailing white flutterings that pollute the dawn. A smoke pit of determined outrage broods in a jail cell, at a kitchen table, against the skin of a diary, a text.

Giant place of happenings, the city spins life that is fast and radical. It is a place of exploration, full of streets that you have never been down. It houses enough of us to swell a revolution, but feeds us enough gasoline to keep our lawns placated and our air conditioners on full steam ahead, Progress! It is earthquake proof, caressed by bicycles, planned by creative dreamers. The model outwits the finished product. Leaves are leafier in ad space; walls are free.

In our first quiet stirrings as modern man we accepted the logic of home here, work there, with the car a line of traffic in between. We bought the dream and then sold it to Asia for the right to crack open fortune cookies and believe what was written therein. Our future, the motor car choked by ivy like it is a throat.

A placard cries in the night, held up by a child. In the night. In the burning city. In the glow of a siren. In the crumbling ruins of a riot. Even as the sweeping tail of history's dress parades on through. In among the ivy. In the back pack. In the hood. In the eyes that turn to look when the light of the cell phone comes flooding in.

There is a rising. A quiet but steady rising, like a swift hush, a hum rising from the throats in the crowd. Bare throats, careless throats, with nothing left to lose.

There is a rising like a singing, like a dreaming, like a coming. The city gets capped, spun away, off into the ether to make do with nothing. It spins there, unsure where to go next, what valley to land in, what river to park beside. And all the boarded-up houses cry out to the refugees that wait in their tent cities, eternal patients smacking at the dusty horrors in their dreaming heads. And all the long hallways and regal staircases cry out to the homeless that live without any rooms at all. "Come to me," they cry. "Storm my gates." And all the pesticide-perfect lawns and golf courses shudder out their long blankets right down to the ocean to catch the fleeing men and women and children before they wash up on the coast of some postcard.

Forty-Nine

CAIUS CESTIUS WAKES to the sound of Piranesi scratching out a living in his living room.

"You still here?"

"I am."

"What's that you're drawing?"

"Your pyramid."

"Am I dead?"

"You've been dead for years."

"Brilliant. You are capturing the essence of the future and the past in one etching."

"I am."

"What is it about my pyramid that you like so much?"

"Its pyramidal shape."

"Anything else?"

"Its indecision. Does it want to be part of the graveyard or part of the river of traffic? No one knows."

"Are tourists kissing it?"

"Always."

Cestius' pet chimp swaggers into the room carrying a handful of peach flesh. She spots the floor with its juice. One, two, three drops. It sits there, the juice, in its circular splendour, and becomes part of history.

"Come here," coos Cestius. "Come here, my love."

The chimp climbs up onto his lap and begins gumming the peach treat. He brought her back from Africa on his last raid. She is the jewel of his life. He suspects that he loves her more than his own wife, more even than his three children. Her back flips never cease to amuse him.

Scratching her lightly on her back he looks at Piranesi and smiles. Piranesi holds up his camera, zooms in on their two faces, and clicks the shutter.

Hilda, Jorgen and Dr. Grebing enter, flapping across the floor in their borrowed sandals. Hilda hikes her toga up to her knees so that we can see that her legs are unshaven, revolutionary.

"When are you going to free the slaves?" she asks, not bothering to say hello first. "We want to know."

"When I'm dead. What's it to you?" asks Cestius, smiling at Piranesi as if they are in the same club.

The chimp gets down off his lap and moves to a corner of the room. She curls up into a fetal position. She's not a fan of Hilda's brassy hair.

"'Who, then, was Cestius, and what is he to me?'" Hilda recites, staring off at the ceiling.

"Why not free them now?" asks Dr. Grebing. "They've completed the pyramid. The deal was that once they'd completed it, you'd set them free."

"I know, I know. But then I'd have to actually do stuff. You know, pick up after myself, prepare my own sandwiches before the Super Bowl, crack my own beers. No fun. Right, Giovanni?"

"Well, I do all that stuff for myself. And now Hannah has me traveling to Germany once a week to have absurd conversations with Hilda, usher Mia in and out of trouble, and even prepare to-scale instruments and foodstuffs for my beggars and waifs. I don't have any slaves to help me with that."

"Really? None at all?"

"No, none."

"And nor do I," says Hilda, putting her hands on her hips and glaring at him.

"Where will they go when I free them? They're like children. They need my council flats. They need my coupons and fare deals. They need my layers and layers of bad debt pressing on their chests while they try to fall asleep at night."

"They don't need anything from you but a raise in minimum wage, better job security, longer maternity leave, free daycare, and Swedish gender neutrality."

"They're asking for way too much, those lazy buggers. Why don't they just do what Piranesi's people do and pose for a living? Giovanni, do you need any workers?"

"Mine are protected by a union. The Tiny Figures Union."

"Bastards!"

Hilda walks over to Cestius and sits down on the sofa beside him. Grapes descend, hanging from a hook suspended on wire, and bump against her face like a joke. She tries to eat them with her mouth alone, but finds herself eating air, mouthing the skin only. She is unaccustomed to the gadgets of the rich.

"I am so tired," she says. "I haven't finished my masterpiece. I haven't brushed my teeth since page one. What have I eaten? Anything?"

"We had some tea on one page," pipes in Bill, who as always is doing a crossword puzzle in the corner.

"Well, I'm starving. I'd die for two slices of gluten, some grated lactose, and a member of the nightshade family, thinly sliced."

"Wouldn't we all," moans Piranesi. "I'd do anything to get

her to go to a research library and do more than just chew pencils, arch her eyebrows, and let coy smiles spread across her face like cliché butter."

"And what about the beach?" asks Jorgen. "She's just stolen that from Kate Chopin. On a bad day. And Anne Carson gave her the last twenty pages of inspiration."

"And that scene where I threw rocks at Violet," says Bill. "I'd never do anything like that. Who would?"

"I would," says Violet, stepping out from behind a column wearing Elizabeth Taylor's head.

"You did!"

"Yep."

Florence comes in as Cestius' wife, dutiful but secretly scheming to overthrow him with Stephen, her young, oiled pin-up lover, but not for a second fudging her lines or moving out of character.

"The slaves are at the gates demanding that you set them free," she says, Stephen nodding agreement beside her. "They have a hankering for freedom. They want to run through the boulevards and congregate in the squares. It would wake us all up. It would bring the tourists to their knees. It would halt the traffic, which would temporarily soothe my asthmatic lungs. I gasp for freedom from technological advancement."

"Alright, for god's sake! Let's do this thing!" shouts Cestius. "Let's all go out there and see what they have in store for us."

"Wait," says Violet. "We're here together. All of us." The characters look around at each other, scan the room, register Cestius' darling pet and the grapes, feel the flimsiness of the columns, built on budget, last minute. "Now what?"

"I figure that *Vedute di Roma* must be playing in a theatre somewhere. Matinee anyone?" says the doctor. "Popcorn's on me."

"No. We've got a lot of cleaning up to do," says Florence, ever the nightingale of goody-two-shoe-ism.

ON LEARNING OF THEIR FREEDOM, Cestius' slaves scatter out into the city. They are found later, posing in sensible triptychs against graffiti that is sometimes beautiful.

It's a simple procedure and never takes more than a few minutes. A slight knick in the skin of a system and the bloodletting begins. Within moments, the whole set is free of the shame of slavery. It quivers with relief.

"HERE," SAYS PIRANESI, passing around a postcard. "This is my favourite place in Rome. Cestius' Pyramid." The characters see the tiny figures' eyes trailing up into the stone heavens, looking for the mythological sense of it all.

"The city is a character here," says Hilda.

"Rome?" asks Bill.

"Of course," says Piranesi.

"But London is where Violet and Bill are from," says Mia, who has returned from her stint as a Thai mermaid.

"Is Heidelberg a town or a city?" asks Jorgen.

"You should know," says Hilda. "You live there."

"I live here," says Jorgen. "I'm part of this book, remember?"

"Barely," says Violet. "What have you done here? You've joined a cult for good measure, fucked a cousin for Thomas Hardy, and been forgiven the sins of all men because she made the mistake of telling someone she'd make this a novel with some nice men in it."

"I don't feel nice."

Hilda goes over to Jorgen and puts her arms around him.

She doesn't mind that the others are watching this show of affection. She needs to be in his arms again.

He feels her flat stomach press against his own.

"Where's the baby?" he asks.

"Oh, that."

"Yes, that. Did you have it already? Without me there?"

"No. Of course not."

"Are you ever going to have it?" asks Florence, genuinely concerned.

"I'm not sure," says Hilda, taking off her red wig and handing it to Violet. "Here. Have this."

Underneath, Hilda's real hair is dishwater blonde *à la* Prince. Her pixie ears are more pronounced. She's not the red-haired devil nurse after all. In fact, she's not even a nurse. She's a writer.

"Thank you. All of you," she says, hugging each character one by one, each person. She lingers a little to say her goodbyes, then steps out into the German countryside, unzips her one-man tent and tumbles inside.

SHE RUSTLES. She crinkles. She simmers in her zippered cocoon. She listens for the quiet puff of goose down settling in her sleeping bag. The warmth embraces her like a mother, like a warm bath after playing dead in a stream. Her privilege is upon her like a stolen gift.

She could stay here, in the belly of the whale.

Or she could jump up, her energy explosion generated by the sap of an uprising, slide through the flapping rupture in her tent and join the storming crowd.

Thank you to all those that talk writing with me, particularly Jessica Asch, Jeremy Beaulne, Thea Bowering, Kirsten Carthew, Caroline Chartier, Corinna Chong, Tamas Dobozy, Sean Johnston, Kim Kinikin, Rebecca Keillor, Stacey Malysh, Kevin McPherson, Amy Modahl, Cecily Nicholson, Anakana Schofield, Glen Stosic, and Michael Tregebov.

Special thanks to Spoke, my writing clan: Natalie Appleton, Michelle Doege, Kristin Froneman, Kerry Gilbert, Karen Meyer, and Laisha Rosnau.

Thank you to my Creative Writing students in both Salmon Arm (2013–14) and Vernon (2015–16).

Thank you to Mike Kelly for saying, "You draw like these guys!" and to Kerry Gilbert for saying, "Send it!"

Thank you to Rolf Maurer for his kindness and wit, and to Mike Leyne for his encouragement, and to both for their fine editing. Thank you to Oliver McPartlin for his wonderful design work.

Thank you to my family. My mum, Adrienne, and my dad, Clifton. To my sisters, Holi and Rachael, my brothers, Dylan and Reuben. All their partners. All their children. And my Barcelona family, especially Yaya Lola, Zoe Holden, and Laura Capelli.

Extra special thanks to Sergi, my big lovey, and Lola, my little lovey.